L Is For...

L Is For...

Credits

Editor: Jayne Fereday
Cover: Fereday Design

All proceeds from this anthology will be given to the RUComingOut charity
www.rucomingout.com

TABLE OF CONTENTS

ALPACA MOONLIGHT
VG Lee

IT WAS A WARM afternoon, late summer, a few years ago. I was sitting on my straight friend Deirdre's patio, which is small but raised to give a very distant sea view. Deirdre insists this adds at least another twenty thousand pounds to the value of her tiny terraced house.

"I'm off to London tomorrow," I'd said. "A book launch at Foyles."

"Foyles? Is that like...Ikea?" She bundled her sheaf of curly hair onto the top of her head and secured it with some garden twine.

"No. It's a very big bookshop covering several floors. The author is Elfrida Greenlawne." I'd smiled self-consciously. "She's a notable feminist lesbian."

"Never heard of her." Deirdre adopted the sneer in both tone and facial expression she only ever adopts when talking about poor people, ugly people, smelly people and almost anyone who belongs to or works in a library.

I persevered. "Think Sarah Waters – only rural setting."

"Never heard of her either. What about Dan Brown? I've heard of him."

"He's not a feminist lesbian."

"Your point being?" Deirdre said.

We hadn't been getting on since the evening I'd announced that I wanted to be a more visible lesbian and not just *her* best friend.

Deirdre had looked up from unwrapping a Cadbury's Creme Egg and said, "What's wrong with being my best friend?"

"Nothing, but you have Martin and Lord Dudley." (Deirdre's partner and cat.) "It's only natural that I should want a woman to share my life with."

"Dude," she waved the Creme Egg at me, "I'd rather eat my own foot than get close up and personal with another woman."

"That's because you're straight."

Deirdre said, "I am what I am," but she'd looked offended.

Back in her garden she began to spray the foxgloves coming up between the paving stones with weed killer.

I said, "Foxgloves are wild flowers not weeds."

"Well they're dead wild flowers now," she said. "I'll meet you at the bookshop."

"But you don't know where it is."

"Then tell me. It's no big deal, is it?"

And yet I'd felt that for her it *was* actually quite a big deal. Deirdre was perfectly at home in M&S, Debenhams and Evans Outsize, perfectly at home in Born-to-Dye-Young where she had her blonde highlights enhanced each month, but Deirdre in London, in a book shop, surrounded by shelves of just...books, that was well outside her comfort zone.

Four rows of chairs were arranged in a semi-circle. On a small table, copies of Elfrida Greenlawne's new novel, 'Alpaca Moonlight', were stacked next to a black and white photograph of the author hugging a sheep.

I sat down in the back row as the all-female audience began to drift in. Here was a club that I didn't yet belong to. I'd dressed carefully. Under normal circumstances I wear a bra but no bra that evening. 'Let it all hang loose,' I'd told my reflection. Just in case it was all hanging a little too loosely, I'd added several, concealing layers in pea-green, topped with a roomy knitted cardigan.

Several women browsed the shelves. Why hadn't I browsed the shelves? What could be more natural than a lesbian browsing a shelf of lesbian literature?

The audience quietened as a large woman wearing a fuchsia pink trouser suit, matching suede bootees and carrying several *John Lewis* carrier bags made her way determinedly towards the woman organising the event.

My neighbour turned to me. "That must be the author. She looks nothing like her photograph."

"Actually that's my friend Deirdre," I said.

The organiser had made the same mistake. Holding out her hand she advanced on Deirdre.

Deirdre ignored her.

The organiser tried again. "Thank you so much for coming all the way from your small-holding in the shadow of the Malvern Hills."

Like an embattled wild animal Deirdre glared fiercely at the audience.

I stood up and waved. "Deirdre, over here."

She picked up the chair put out for Elfrida Greenlawne and carried it shoulder high to where I was sitting in the back row.

"Budge up so I can get this chair in next to my friend," Deirdre told the woman sitting next to me.

Reluctantly the woman budged up.

Elfrida Greenlawne looked exactly like her photo. She wore a large pullover, faded cotton trousers and muddy boots. Her hair was admirably wild, tangled and tawny.

Deirdre whispered, "That woman's not been near a comb in decades."

Thirty minutes later – inspired – I was on my feet, clapping and cheering. My mind was full of possibilities that had never occurred to me before. Should I go on a fell walking holiday? Could I sunbathe topless and swim in icy rock pools? Was it too late to take up kick-boxing, bee-keeping, plant husbandry?

I turned to say, "Wasn't she great?" but Deirdre was already several feet away picking up a book from a display of...

She flipped the book open in the middle. "Eeugh! Gross! Dude, I'm bringing up my breakfast."

...lesbian erotica.

She tossed it back on the shelf. Head on one side she began to read out book titles: "Hot Lesbian Erotica, Best Lesbian Bondage Erotica, Vampire Erotica, Five Minute Erotica—"

"Deirdre—"

"The Mammoth Encyclopaedia of Erotica, The Golden Age of Lesbian Erotica – don't you lesbians have any other interests?"

"It's a display of lesbian erotica."

"It's not for me, dude. I'll meet you in Pizza Hut."

I bought my signed copy of 'Alpaca Moonlight' and set off after her. By the time I reached Pizza Hut, she'd already filled her bowl from the salad bar and one for me too, heavy on the croutons the way she knows I like.

I sat down.

Out of the side of her mouth, Deirdre said, "Don't look now but that lezzer who didn't want to budge up has just followed you in."

"Hello again," the woman said stopping at our table. "Elfrida Greenlawne was terrific, wasn't she?"

"She was shite," Deirdre answered.

I kicked her under the table.

"A total loser. Small-holding in the shadow of the Malvern Hills...my backside. What she needs," Deirdre stabbed a quarter of hard-boiled egg, "is for some big hairy-arsed bloke to give her a good shagging." She looked at me. "And you can stop kicking me under the table because this is a free country and I'm entitled to my opinion."

Two Deirdre-less years passed. I found a girlfriend. We went on a fell walking holiday and I bathed in an icy pool and came down with pleurisy. While recovering my girlfriend met someone else. I joined a kick-boxing class but may never go topless or keep bees etc. In all this activity I didn't once glimpse Deirdre – not even a sighting in Born-to-Dye-Young having her highlights, highlighted. And then one morning, just before nine, my bus was stuck in traffic on the High Street. I noticed that Marks & Spencer were having a summer sale. Their double doors were still locked but a large blonde haired woman was ramming the glass with her shoulder. Inside the store a sales assistant was shaking her head and pointing at her watch.

Deirdre, (of course it had to be Deirdre) took a step backwards. I thought she was about to walk away but instead she bellowed, "Dude, will you open this fucking door?"

As the bus finally sped off, I thought back to that evening in Foyles – Deirdre carrying chair and carrier bags towards me, through the rows of women so unlike herself. I remembered thinking that she'd looked like an embattled wild animal. Yes, she was rude, homophobic, thoroughly nasty, but what sort of friend had I been? I'd never given a thought to how she was feeling, not just then, but from the moment I'd told her that being *her* best friend just wasn't enough.

The next day, I headed into London and Deirdre's spiritual home - the bed linen department in *John Lewis's*. I've always been drawn to anything floral and at that moment I felt I desperately needed a floral hit. And there it was. Perfect. Egyptian cotton, 600 thread - pink tea-roses.

In my head I seemed to hear Deirdre's voice. "Step away from that bedding."

My hand reached out to pluck the duvet set from the rack.

"Leave it!"

The voice was at my shoulder. I turned. "Deirdre!"

She held up her hand. "Love means never having to say you're sorry."

"I wasn't intending to say sorry."

"Me neither."

She looked different. She'd styled her curls into a smooth French pleat and wore a tailored trouser suit.

Deirdre twirled. "I'm a feminist now. Actually my Martin says I've always been a feminist as in," she held her telescopic umbrella in front of her face as if it was a microphone and sang, "*I am strong, I am invincible. I am wo-man.* Love that word 'invincible'. Who'd have thought someone would stick it in a lyric? Martin says whoever it was should publish a book on how to write a blockbuster hit."

It was as if there'd been no two-year break in our friendship. I put the duvet set back on the shelf. By unspoken mutual agreement we set off in search of a cafeteria.

Standing side-by-side on the escalator heading upwards, Deirdre said, "I saw you once in that bookshop. You were buying an arm load of books. Afterwards I went up to the assistant and said, 'Dude, I'll take whatever that woman in the shapeless cardigan bought.'."

###

VG LEE is an author and stand-up comedian. She was born in Birmingham but has gradually worked her way southwards and now lives and writes in Hastings on the Sussex coast. She has published four novels and a collection of short stories. In 2012, her most recent novel, *Always you, Edina*, was chosen as Stonewall's Book of the Month for June. A few months later Lee was also nominated for a Stonewall Award for writing.

Her other novels are: *The Comedienne*, Diva Books, 2001, *The Woman in Beige*, Diva Books, 2003, *Diary of a Provincial Lesbian*, Onlywomen Press, 2005 and *Always you, Edina*, Ward Wood Publishing, 2012. www.wardwoodpublishing.co.uk

The short story collection, *As You Step Outside,* was published in 2008 by Tollington Press.

VG Lee's work has appeared in Chroma, Magma, Poetry Review, Mslexia and many anthologies. She has also contributed humorous articles to The Lady magazine, www.lady.co.uk and Gaze – A Modern Review, www.gaze-amodernreview.co.uk.

In 2009, to celebrate her sixtieth year, VG Lee decided to become a stand-up comedian. She set herself a target of performing at sixty venues. Sixty became ninety and she finished the year as a runner-up in the prestigious Hackney Empire's New Act of the Year 2010. She has appeared twice at the Edinburgh Festival. In 2013, she performed her one-woman play, *Lady of the Wild West Hill* to packed audiences as part of the Brighton Fringe. She is a regular at many lgbtq events including Polari at the Southbank, Northampton's BooQfest and LFest. She won Author of the Year 2014 at the Planet London Lesbian Oscars.

I REALLY DID LOVE HER
Suzanne Egerton

"FUCK, FUCK, and buckets of bollocks!"

"What's up, Lozza?" I called from my supine position in the centre of the sunbeam, 'Easy Like Sunday Morning' playing in my head. It was an effort. The Comic Cuts section of the paper slid from my relaxed fingers and whispered to the floor. Motes of airborne dust hung in the sunbeam. What if each were a tiny world, inhabited by a billion nano-beings, each with a tiny life to lead, each with its tiny concerns? Would that make me God, I wondered? I guessed not; their God would care for each and every one of them, allowing them their choices, and keeping an eye on things as they floated in their squillions across the sunbeam. The role of the devil might suit me better. Drunk with power, I waved a languid hand through the air, causing the infinitesimal specks to churn. A villainous cackle left my throat.

"N'ya-ha-haaar," I gloated. "That'll teach you lot who really controls things around here, you puny poltroons!"

"Shall I call Psychiatric Services now, or leave it till after lunch?" demanded my lover, her glorious cloud of red-gold hair lightly brushing my brow as she leant over me. Astonishing how that cobweb touch could awaken my lazy body all of a sudden - or part thereof, anyway. I reached up towards the hidden fissure in the crinkly cheesecloth between the buttons of her shirt and got half-smothered with a cushion for my trouble.

"Randy bastard," accused my attacker, without pity. My sunbeam universe experienced its own chaos theory moment as I sat up and attempted to pull her down on to my lap. She writhed as if to escape, giggling and letting her hair tumble over her face; and then consented, leaning her head against mine.

"It's all right for you, Mel," she said. "I've reached a really sticky point in this essay, and it's doing my bloody head in."

"Poor baby, you need a break from it," I soothed, stroking her gently and trying to establish by touch whether her Sunday throw-ons concealed underwear or not.

"Chancer!" she laughed, slapping my hands away. She rose and lifted my empty coffee cup. It was a great floral bucket of a cup, the gritty dregs still smelling like boulevard cafes. I followed her into the kitchen and nuzzled under her hair to kiss the back of her neck, my arms around her waist as she washed the cups.

"Perhaps I can help;" I said. "I could do some of your research on the laptop. Two brains have got to be better than one, hmm?"

This was actually code for, "If we get this shit sorted in the next hour or so, you might feel entitled to some afternoon delight..." But she knew me too well.

"That's your Sunday brain you're so generously offering, I take it?" she enquired. "So I end up with an essay littered with double entendres and sexual references? Yes, that'll go down well with old Po-face Professor Peyton. Thanks, but no thanks." I groaned. "If you really want to be a help," she added, "go and pick us up a pizza for lunch."

"Yeah, ok," I sighed.

"Anything with mushrooms on it!" she called, as she disappeared back into the spare room to resume the task.

The work must have gone well. Either that or maybe a block set in for the day, because a couple of hours later we lay on the big patchwork quilt, laughing and tussling as the sun tried to penetrate the drawn blinds. We rolled like puppies, until passion overtook play, and we tangled and slithered against each other, until just the holding, and the quiet breathing of satiety became enough.

My God, she was beautiful. Like most women, she had ridiculous concerns about her body, which no amount of reassurance could totally dispel. About the towering intellect there was no false modesty; but the wonderful body I worshipped and longed to immortalise, to fix in time on a life-sized canvas, fell inexplicably

14

short of some unknowable standard she set it. As for me, I never tired of gazing at her, studying her, after we had had our fill of each other's body. Her face always looked that way, dewy and fresh, even in the mornings. I loved the pale blue eyes with their thick sandy lashes, the flawless bone structure, the creamy skin with its dusting of freckles. She seldom wore make-up: she didn't need to.

I suppose I remember that particular day because it was the last of our golden Sundays. Up until then, the wonderful weekends tended to follow each other like a vivid slide show. On Friday night we would celebrate with a couple of bottles of wine, and there would be sex for breakfast on a Saturday if I was lucky. Funny, how her mouth always tasted of warm croissants and marmalade. Then food shopping for the week, coffee at Flavio's, and perhaps lunch at one of the cafe bistros that characterised our city village. In the afternoon she would write or research, a stack of books tottering beside the computer, whilst I watched sport on the telly or listened to music. Sometimes we went out later to eat with friends or to a rock concert; sometimes we experimented with home cuisine, usually with acceptably edible results.

Sundays, though, were the highlight of my week, the one day when I had her all to myself. Even reading the papers in silence together was deeply pleasurable, and the leisurely pace of our frequent sexual activity reflected the ease and comfort of the day.

I really did love her.

However, as her academic nemesis approached, I owned less and less of her time. The piles of A4, heavy with my lover's thoughts and reasoning, grew fat in their folders; her self-discipline was staggering. My longing for her body as for her attention was forcibly suppressed, after many gently offhand rebuffs. It was all very well for me, she told me; I had prostituted *my* gifts and was doing very well out of it. Ruefully, I had to accept that this was true. *My* nine-to-five was devoted to the sculpting and casting of supposedly collectable wildlife figures. These fancies kept the mortgage paid very adequately, as they left their clean shapes in the dust on retailers' glass shelves everywhere. A new woodland birds series was being advertised currently in weekend magazines, and already thousands from this range were flying into chintzy homes to fill the empty nests there. Though far from rich, I made far more than the average artist – I still thought of myself as an artist – and simply had to keep the flow of furry and feathery love objects coming. When the collectables first took off I had planned to rent a proper studio, to explore the far reaches of my talent, and try to sell the results through established galleries. Somehow I never got around to it. The creeping effect of adequate success numbed both ambition and creativity, and I found myself too busy with my conveyor belt editions to think about Art.

So now, contained by Saturday's new shape, I sauntered the aisles of the supermarket alone with a list provided for me and decayed quietly in front of the television all day and evening. I cooked the odd meal and spent Sunday mornings in bed, followed by pointless pints in various local pubs.

Never mind, I told myself, the finals would soon be over, and things could go back to their old, satisfying way.

Nobody was surprised at Lol's good degree with Honours, and I remember marvelling at the way the spotlights gave her a shimmering halo as she crossed the stage to receive her scroll. Ridiculous tears blurred my vision as she glanced towards the seat block where she knew I was sitting and smiled her sweet and confident smile.

Afterwards, we enjoyed a holiday in the sun. There are some photos I still have somewhere, brilliance and brightness leaping from the shiny surfaces: the impossibly blue sky, the white buildings; her brown limbs, the hippy-style muslin dress she wore. Her hair. Her smile. Life's turning wheel on hold for the virtual evermore. It was perfect. Love, and sun, and velvet nights.

Perfect.

That autumn, she left me.

I guess I must have been a real pain in the arse when she told me she was going for a second, more difficult degree. She had set her sights on an academic career, with possibly a professorship some years down the line. She settled into a new rhythm of study and lectures, and I found myself becoming moody and distant, falling into a pattern of passive aggression. I was mourning the loss of her, even while her physical presence taunted me with its continuing allure. We talked, of course. That is, whenever I failed to come up with an avoidance tactic. And when we talked, my inner anger made me monosyllabic and unhelpful. She took to going out with college friends, and not being at home at weekends for one reason or another. I accused her of infidelity and was uncharacteristically vindictive. Only someone who knows the deepest sensitivities of another can be as spiteful as I became at that time. Of course the real, transparent object of my corrosive jealousy was her relationship with her work, but I couldn't admit it to myself, let alone to her.

So of course, she left.

For a while I drank too much and had rather too many one-night stands; the usual thing. Just getting her out of my system. But it's now a couple of years on and I'm well over it. I've had a number of relationships, though nothing long-term. The women I tend to go for are articulate, intelligent, and of course physically attractive, but any suggestion of moving in together gets short shrift from me; the words "You won't commit," have hung in the air as more than one door has closed behind me. But that's OK. Once bitten, and all that.

There's even an upside to the story. I've sold up and invested in a small two-storey premises to replace my old workshop, with room for a studio and a modest gallery on the ground floor, and a flat above. Money will be tight, but it doesn't matter. It's months since I produced a new cutesy figurine, and I've been working instead on some substantial abstract canvases. I've even completed a medium-sized sculpture, of a beggar – it's reasonably good, I think. A couple of talented art school graduates have asked for wall space, and a craft jeweller has shown some interest. The gallery should be ready to open by Christmas, and I've got to admit, I'm quite excited about it, even though sleep is on the back burner for a bit, what with working on pieces for the launch. A mate of mine is doing the lighting, and I've been helping with that too, along with basic stuff like sanding the floor, erecting partitions, etcetera.

I've also started to paint a life-sized nude of Lol, the portrait she'd never let me do. I think I've got the beautiful skin-tone, and the wonderful hair is coming along quite well, but her smile is elusive as yet. There's no rush; I might decide to keep it anyway if it turns out all right. I'll finish it off once the gallery gets going, and then make up my mind.

Funnily enough, one of our old friends stopped me in the street the other day. She – Lol that is – has moved to Brighton, seemingly. She will eventually get her doctorate or whatever, there's no doubt of that. I wonder what she'd think about my dynamic change of direction. I'd like to think she'd be pleased for me, and even a bit impressed, perhaps.

There now, you see, Professor Lorraine Anderson, I did it. I finally got off my arse and did it, and without you, too.

But anyway, best of luck. I won't forget you.

###

SUZANNE EGERTON'S random career path has zigged up to doorsteps with cleaning products and zagged through jewellery shops and casinos. She is currently a fitness instructor, and lives in Motherwell. Her first novel, *Out Late with Friends and Regrets*, was published last year by Paddy's Daddy Publishing. Suzanne loves the scary presence of an audience and has read her work at numerous events, including the Edinburgh International Book Festival. So far she has refrained from throwing up in the wings. She is currently working on a retro novel set against the background of London casinos.

Suzanne Egerton, author of Out Late with Friends and Regrets.

You can find me at Amazon UK, Amazon US, on Facebook and at Paddy's Daddy Publishing.

ALANA MOLTON-CROFT AND ME
Kiki Archer

THIS IS HER, this is her! I stand from my seat in the fancy restaurant and smile broadly at the beautiful brunette walking my way. Wow. No wonder she keeps her profile picture greyed out. Eyes like that must bring her far too much attention. She's smiling, she's smiling. Here goes. I step forwards slightly and reach out my hand. "Hi, I'm…"

Oh. I yank my arm back in as the brunette sashays past and try to lean back down into my seat without anyone noticing. I glance behind me as I pretend to flick my hair, cooling my flushed cheeks in the process. The brunette's being swallowed up by a gaggle of girls, kissing her, hugging her, squeezing her shoulders. Nice shoulders, strong shoulders…

"Poppy Sinclair?"

I spin back around and look up … at Anne Robinson, pre Weakest Link surgery. "Hi," I say, nodding too enthusiastically: overcompensation for the shock of deep disappointment. "Alana?"

"Al-ar-na Molton-Croft."

This is formal. I stand and do a sort of bowing head nod. "Alana Molton-Croft, hi."

"Al-ar-na."

I nod again unsure of quite where it is that I'm going wrong. "Eleanor, shall we sit?"

"Al-ar-na."

Oh for fuck's sake can I just call you Anne? I smile and nod as if I've got it. "This is a really nice place."

Anne Robinson sniffs and takes off her green quilted Cotton Traders jacket. She ignores the hovering maître d' and folds the precious piece of clothing on top of her handbag, which she tucks tightly into the table. I stare at my date. She's wearing a turtle neck,

19

and a brooch. I remind myself to check which box I ticked in the oldest-acceptable-age bracket. "My friend recommended it," I say, again too eagerly, wondering why I feel the need to be liked by this woman. Maybe my previous, also poor, attempts at blind-dating have had more of an effect on me than I like to admit.

"You're pretty."

I sit up straighter in my seat and smile stupidly. "Oh, thank you."

"Alana Molton-Croft likes to compliment."

My smile starts to waver. "Oh thank you."

"Alana Molton-Croft says what she feels."

My smile's gone. I have to say something. "And will Alana Molton-Croft be with us all evening?"

"You're not a fan of third person chatter?"

I shake my head. "I wouldn't say it was one of my favourite pastimes, no."

"Alana Molton-Croft finds it breaks the ice. She thinks we'll be debating the split infinitive in no time."

Well she can bloody think again. Focus, Poppy, we're not even five minutes in. I try and smile at the woman opposite. "That's right. You're an English major."

"Guilty as charged. In fact I have a rather fun little compatibility test that I like to tease my dates with."

I swallow, unsure if it's the prospect of a test that worries me the most, or the notion that Anne Robinson's doppelganger wants to tease me. I watch as my date reaches into her handbag and wish that I was on the table behind where the whoops and giggles from Brunette and her gang sound so much more my style.

"So this really is rather interesting."

I stare at the piece of paper presented to me, with nine random letters written at the top.

"I'm a huge Countdown fan."

Oh god, I shouldn't have lied on my profile. I thought ticking the *likes Sudoku and crosswords* box might give me that extra edge.

"Just shout them out, as and when."

I look at the piece of paper. "The letters?"

"Ha. Pretty and witty, this really is going rather well. So, we can run it all evening, unless you have the nine already that is?"

Oh bugger, she wants me to make up words. I look again. The only thing jumping out at me is … MAN, no wait, there's CAR. I glance up. "Shall we order first?"

"Alana Molton-Croft would like you to whet her appetite with a word."

What? This is turning her on? I open my eyes wider hoping the letters will un-jumble themselves. "ACNE! There's acne!"

Alana reaches over and fingers the letters. "I'm sure we can find you some CREAM for that."

I giggle, spotting another word. "What if it's on my…" I tap the letters "…ARSE."

Alana frowns. "Shall we order?"

The majority of the meal was eaten in silence, apart from the moment I found the word SNORER. I felt it warranted a toast and guzzled more wine in self-congratulations. Alana Molton-Croft didn't look up from her cheese and biscuits.

"So," I say, taking the receipt from the maître d', "it was lovely to meet you, Alana."

"Romancer."

"No, I just think whoever books pays."

"Romancer."

I'm temporarily distracted from Anne Robinson's come on by Brunette and the gaggle of girls passing our table. It sounds like they're heading to the dancing bar opposite. Wait, did Brunette just look at me? Was that a look? Was that an *I hope you're coming to the dancing bar* look? And an *I hope that woman's your mother* look? My four Pinot Grigios get the better of me. "Well if you think it's gone well we could always head to a bar and dance for a bit?"

"Oh for goodness sake, Poppy, romancer is the eight letter word, so give me the nine."

I scan the bloody piece of paper one final time. "Romancers. The nine letter word is romancers."

"We are rather, aren't we?"

"I passed?"

"Not swimmingly, but I like the idea of dancing. Slight intellectual mismatch, but physically we could explode."

"Right," I say, standing from my seat, "bring on the dancing challenge."

"No challenges, just synchronicity. Our bodies need to work together."

I watch as my date zips herself into her green quilted jacket. "You're good at dancing?" I ask.

"They call me Shakira."

The dance club is empty, apart from Brunette and her gaggle of girls who are spilling out of a corner booth. It's Monday; who comes dancing on a Monday? Oh my good god, Shakira does. I stare at the centre of the room. Anne Robinson on speed. She's body popping. Oh wait, what's this? A moon walk? With an added funky-chicken head cluck? Damn, and her bottom's twerking too? I place our drinks down on the table, unsure of quite what to do. I glance at the gaggle of girls who are all nodding at my date with respect. I can't compete with that. I can't even keep up with that. Oh bugger she's calling me over.

"She's quite something, isn't she?"

I turn around. Brunette's talking. She's talking to me. "Mmm." I nod, unable to form any words.

"Are you two…?"

"No, no, no, no, no!" I wonder why my voice is suddenly so high pitched.

Brunette's smiling. "That's good then."

I can't help but stare. Those eyes. Those lips. Whose hands are they? My hips suddenly start gyrating, forced around and around by Anne Robinson's rather persistent punnany.

"Alana Molton-Croft would like to dance."

I watch with dismay as Brunette walks back to the booth. My hips are still moving but now my arms are out to the side, warm fingers entwined in my own. We're doing some sort of Mexican wave. Come on, Poppy, you can do this. Show Brunette and her girls your moves. I spin around and face my date. I need to take back control. The beat's good so I start with some fist pumps, forcing Alana to give me some space.

"Aggressively attractive, I like it."

I watch my date copy my move. God, we must look like such knobs. I need to change it up. I decide to add in a jump. The jumping fist pump. Alana copies me again. Fine, I'll do the carwash. I start to circle my outstretched palm. In fact I'll do the double carwash. Both of my palms now polishing away. Alana starts polishing too. Oh for fuck's sake, I'll do the finger pointer then. I point up, down, side to side.

Alana stands still. "Shall we just do our own thing?"

Oh. I lower my finger and watch as she starts the self-molest. Her hands caressing up and down her own body. Who knew a woman in a turtle neck could look so sexy? I start the side step and wonder if I should get my drink. Wait, Brunette and her gang are coming over. They're dancing. They're smiling. And look, the lights are changing. It's darker. Wow, I love Ultra-Violet. Look at Brunette's smile glowing, and her friend's white jeans. I catch sight of myself in a mirror. Oh what the fuck are those white specks on my shoulders? I glance down. My black top's covered. It can't be dandruff. I don't have dandruff. Damn, it looks like dandruff. I start the shoulder sweep.

Alana steps behind me and brushes my back. "Is that just dust?"

I laugh too loudly, catching another glimpse of myself in the mirror. One front tooth is shining out at me. My false one. My crown. It's glowing like a fluorescent peg. I look like Nanny McPhee.

"Come on. Let's show these ladies what we've got." Alana spins me around and thrusts her leg between mine.

I try not to open my mouth. I have to keep peg tooth under wraps. I make "Mm hm" sounds as I try to get into her crotch grinding rhythm. She's moving us up and down. Crikey I shouldn't have worn my tight trousers. I glance at the girls. Brunette's looking. She's smiling. I smile. Oh fuck, peg tooth's on show. I jam my mouth closed and look back at my date. I try to speak without showing my teeth. "Shall we shit?"

"Pardon?"

Damn, who knew you couldn't say sit without showing your teeth? I whisper into her ear instead. "Sit? Drinks?"

Alana keeps her leg between mine. "I'm rather enjoying the grinding. Let me ramp up the pace."

"No, no."

"Let's take it lower then." Alana suddenly bends her knees, forcing me down with her. I don't hear the rip, but I do feel the rush of cold air entering the back of my trousers. I break free from Shakira and pull myself back up. That's when I see it. In the mirror. My white thong, lit up like a glow stick. I stagger backwards off the dance floor and press myself firmly against a wall.

"Are you ok? Did I hurt you?"

The UV lights are still on and my false tooth is still glowing. "No, no. I think I'll just head home."

"We've not had our drinks yet." Alana looks genuinely disappointed. "It was the grinding wasn't it? It was too much. I promise you I wasn't trying to come."

My lips betray me and my teeth are on full show. "Err, I do think I'll go."

"Well I'll go too then." Alana reaches for her jacket and handbag. "After you."

"No, no."

"You want to stay?"

"No, no, you lead out."

Alana walks towards the exit and I sort of wobble my way behind her, pretending to stretch, one hand covering my bottom.

The glow of the street is nice, and not at all fluorescent. I smile, more relaxed, despite the draught. "I've had a good night. Thank you, Alana."

"It's such a shame that we don't work physically either."

Oh, I thought I had it on the dancing. I nod. "Yes. So, this is goodbye."

"Poppy Sinclair, I think it is." Alana smiles. "It was nice to meet you too."

We hug briefly.

"Bye."

"Bye."

We both start to walk. Damn, it's that awkward moment when you walk away in the same direction.

"Excuse me!"

I spin around, quickly hiding the hole in my trousers. It's Brunette! She's looking at us.

"I was just wondering if I could have your number?"

I smile, elated by this turn of events. I look at Alana who's smiling too. She's fine with it. "Of course," I say.

Brunette shifts awkwardly. "Sorry, no." She steps past me. "I just haven't been able to take my eyes off you all evening."

My date straightens her green quilted jacket. "Alana Molton-Croft is pleased to hear that. Do you by chance like Countdown?"

KIKI ARCHER is a UK-based, best-selling, award-winning author. Her debut novel, *But She Is My Student*, won the UK's 2012 SoSoGay Best Book Award. Its sequel, *Instigations*, took just twelve hours from its release to reach the top of the Amazon lesbian fiction chart; and Kiki's third novel, *Binding Devotion*, was a finalist in the 2013 Rainbow Awards. Kiki's fourth offering, *One Foot Onto The Ice*, has been her most successful to date, breaking into the American Amazon contemporary fiction top 100 as well as achieving the US and UK Amazon lesbian fiction number one. The sequel, *When You Know,* went straight to number one on the Amazon UK, Amazon America and Amazon Australia lesbian fiction charts, as well as number one on the iTunes, Smashwords and Lulu Gay and Lesbian chart. Kiki was crowned the Ultimate Planet's Independent Author of the Year in 2013 and received an honourable mention in the 2014 Author of the Year awards dubbed the #LesbianOscars. She has sold 35,000 copies of her novels to date and is taking a well-earned break from writing as she works on her very first screenplay, an adaptation of her debut novel, *But She Is My Student.*

Check out Kiki's author readings and other videos on her YouTube channel: www.youtube.com/kikiarcherbooks

Website: www.kikiarcherbooks.com

Twitter: www.twitter.com/kikiarcherbooks

Facebook: www.facebook.com/kiki.archer

LOOKING FOR PRINCESS CHARMING
Deborah Underwood

"...AND THEY ALL lived happily ever after."

Laura closed the book and looked at the faces of the children in Year 2, sitting cross-legged in front of her. Eve was smiling happily and making plaits in the hair of the girl in front of her. Jade was sucking her thumb, whilst Charlie was poking his nose and eating whatever was on his finger. Harry was scratching his head ferociously, and Laura made a mental note to check her own hair later.

"Now I can see mummies and daddies waiting, so go and get your bags and coats and I will see you tomorrow," smiled Laura. The children obediently collected their belongings and Laura stood by the classroom's exterior door, making sure they reached the appropriate adult safely.

Jane, the Year 3 teacher, poked her head around Laura's door. "Fancy a coffee before I attempt to mark the maths test?" Jane entered the classroom and picked up the book Laura had been reading. "Cinderella? Again? Aren't your class fed up with this book yet?"

"No," replied Laura. "They love it."

Jane raised an eyebrow quizzically. "You mean you love it!"

"What can I say? I am a sucker for a happy ending. Happy ever after and all that."

"And how is your happy ever after going?" Jane teased. "Are you closer to finding your Princess Charming?"

Laura blushed. "Oh...you know how hard it is to meet people."

"Did you try that dating website we talked about?" asked Jane.

Laura smiled sheepishly. "Well..."

"Go on," encouraged Jane. "What have you got to lose?"

Laura sipped her latte and turned on her laptop, Jane's word echoing in her ears. It had been just over a year since she left her ex-girlfriend. She should never have got involved, and had done so on the rebound from yet another relationship that had gone sour – not her doing. But Laura was a romantic; she believed in a one true love. So where is she? she wondered.

Right, Laura thought with an air of determination. She logged onto GaydarGirls and began to create her profile. The first hurdle. What shall I call myself? Laura1982 is so boring! What about something more sexy, like, Hotgirl? No. Too much. I am looking for true love, not one night stands. Although... No. Laura shook her head dismissively and focussed on creating her profile.

After a few minutes, Laura decided upon Cinderella82. She added a few personal details. Not too much, she thought. I want them to be interested and eager to know more. Happy with her profile, and with a decisive click of the mouse, her profile went live. Sitting back on her chair, Laura re-read it. "Right Princess Charming, where are you?" she said out loud.

It was Monday morning and Laura was bringing her class into the hall, sitting them in rows, for the morning's assembly.

"Good weekend?" asked Jane as she sat her Year 3s behind Laura's class.

"Yes! I joined that website and I've been chatting to this woman online," whispered Laura hurriedly as she sat down next to her class.

"Oooh! Tell me more later," whispered Jane over Laura's shoulder.

The head teacher entered the hall. "Good morning everyone."

Laura was in the staffroom kitchen, stirring her coffee. She looked over her shoulder and saw that the other members of staff were deep in conversation about the latest changes to the curriculum.

"So...I've been messaging her and she seems really nice, we have the same interests," she told Jane.

"Ok," said Jane, "what does she look like?"

"Well she hasn't put a picture on her profile."

"What? How do you even know 'she' isn't a 'he'?"

"Because she said she isn't out and besides, her profile name is Twinkle," replied Laura.

Jane spat her coffee out. "Twinkle?? What sort of name is that? Find out her real name, and you really need to call her to make sure she is who she says she is. And if you do decide to meet her, for God's sake, meet in a public place!"

"Ok!" said Laura, "I do have a degree, you know!"

"Yes," responded Jane, "but unfortunately, it isn't in common sense."

Laura tucked a stray strand of hair behind her ear as she pressed call on her phone. A female voice answered. "Hello?"

Laura did her best to appear calm and in control, despite the butterflies in her stomach. "Hi, is that Twinkle? I mean Susanne."

"Oh. You need my mum," came the reply.

Laura experienced a moment of panic. She has a daughter! That's ok. I work with children; I like children, she thought as she tried to reassure herself.

Another female voice came onto the phone. This time, Susanne. Laura regained her composure and they agreed to meet at a local pub on Friday night.

Laura took a deep breath, opened the door of the George and the Dragon public house and walked in. It was quite busy and she manoeuvred her way to a space at the bar. Laura ordered a glass of Pinot Grigio. She had spent a long time deciding what to wear this evening, and had settled on skinny jeans, a smart shirt and black boots. She had even straightened her shoulder length brown hair. Laura took her drink and sat at an empty table, facing the door. She sipped her wine nervously. She knew if she drank too fast, it would go straight to her head.

The door opened. Laura looked over anxiously and saw it was a couple who headed towards the bar. She took another sip of wine, relaxing a little.

The door opened again and Laura looked up expectantly. A woman walked over to her, smiling, and said, "Laura?" Laura felt her stomach sink.

Susanne didn't look quite as her profile stated. For one thing, she looked a lot older —about in her mid-fifties, Laura judged. She had a short brown bob and thick-lensed glasses, giving the impression her eyes were bigger than they were. She wore black high heel shoes, a tight, short black skirt and a white blouse showing ample cleavage.

Laura stood up to greet her. Ok, she thought, she is not my type, but I can be polite and enjoy an evening with a fellow lesbian.

"Hi Susanne, it's lovely to meet you. What would you like to drink?" Laura said politely.

"I would love a snowball," replied Susanne.

"Sounds great," said Laura, having no idea what that was. "I'll get you one."

"Thanks babe."

She returned with the drink and saw that Susanne had moved their seats closer together. She took a deep breath and smiling, sat down.

"You're very pretty," said Susanne.

"Thank you," replied Laura.

"Do you do this a lot?" Susanne asked.

"Er. No," Laura replied nervously. "Actually, this is the first internet date I have ever been on."

Susanne reached over and touched Laura's knee.

"Don't be nervous, babe, you'll get used to it."

Laura continued smiling and crossed her legs, forcing Susanne's hand off of her knee.

"Ok babe. Let's get down to the nitty gritty. Have you ever been with a man?"

Laura coughed as a sip of her wine caught in her throat. She gulped. "Well, I don't think that…"

"Thing is I have met a few women online..."

"Really?" said Laura, as her anxiety continued to increase.

"Yeah, and there are a lot of time wasters out there, so I need to make myself clear."

"Right...," said Laura. She continued to smile fixedly.

"My husband says it's ok for me to take a woman as a lover, only he will want to join in too, obviously." Susanne gave Laura a big smile, revealing a row of crooked off-white teeth. She took a sip of her snowball.

Laura continued smiling, her jaws aching. She blinked very slowly and took a large gulp of her wine.

Bang! Bang! Buzz! Buzz!

"Where's the fire?" called a voice inside the house. "I'm coming!"

Jane opened her front door to see Laura standing there.

"Hi Laura," Jane said in surprise. "I thought you had a date tonight?"

"I do," replied Laura.

Jane looked over Laura's shoulder, "Oh! Is she here? Did you bring her with you?"

"No", said Laura, "she is still in the pub."

Jane frowned. "I don't understand. Do you want me to go back with you to meet her? Give her the once over?"

"Oh no!" exclaimed Laura. "Absolutely not. I mean, I said I had to go to the toilet and...well... I have left her there, sitting with a snowball. And I have no idea what kind of drink that even is!"

"A snowball is a...Hold on! Rewind a bit. You did what? Why?"

"Well, I think she is still waiting for me to return from the ladies. She said she wanted a threesome. I panicked, said I needed the loo, and well, here I am," finished Laura lamely.

"Oh sweetheart! Come on in."

Right thought Laura as she opened up her laptop. Jane is right. I cannot let one bad experience put me off. Get back on the horse and all that. Who am I kidding? I will delete my profile.

Ping! A message popped up on her GaydarGirls account. Laura read it:

'Hey Cinderella, you look lovely, and we have lots of things in common. And I know this is forward, but life is short, so do you fancy meeting for lunch?'

The message was from Sporty123. Laura looked at her profile and photo. Sporty 123 was a personal trainer and the photo showed a good looking girl with short brown hair, wearing shorts and a t-shirt, posing on a beach somewhere. Hmm, thought Laura. Maybe I could be tempted to go on another date.

Saturday lunchtime and Laura sat in the pub garden at the Dog and Bone. The weather had turned warmer and the garden was full of people enjoying the sunshine. Laura had put on her new summer dress, Jimmy Choo shoes (specially bought for the occasion) and her Dior sunglasses, hoping to, what was it Madonna said? Strike a pose. She sipped a mojito.

A red sports car pulled up into the car park and Sporty123 got out. Laura looked up and breathed a sigh of relief. At least her date looked like her profile.

Sporty123 walked over to her. She was wearing jeans, a tight white t-shirt and designer shades. She had spiky, short brown hair and a tan. She smiled at Laura, showing a row of perfect, white teeth. "Hi Laura."

Laura's heart skipped a beat. "Hey Jude," she smiled shyly, resisting the urge to start singing. Laura stood up and held out a hand. "It's nice to meet you."

Jude smiled and shook Laura's hand. "Ditto. Would you like another?" she asked, nodding at the mojito.

"Yes please," said Laura.

"And I will get a menu for us."

They ordered food and exchanged pleasantries whilst waiting for their order.

"Great shoes," said Jude to Laura. "My ex had a pair of those."

"Thanks," replied Laura. "I love shoes and I bought these especially for days like these."

"Sunny days or lunch dates?" Jude smiled, flirting.

Laura laughed.

"You see, my ex had everything," Jude said as she took a bite of her veggie burger. "You know, it killed me when she left. She was the love of my life and you never get over something like that." Jude put her burger on her plate and continued to talk. "Soul mates. That was my ex and me. I really don't think I will ever find that kind of love again, you know?"

Laura swallowed a mouthful of her burger and said, "Well, I believe that we meet people for a reason and we will eventually find true love. But then again, I am a romantic."

Jude considered this. "No. My ex was my true love - we had something special. It's something I will never get over." She laughed. "Now, this one time, we..."

Laura listened, continuing to eat. Jude did not seem to stop for breath and her burger remained untouched on her plate.

Laura felt her hope starting to slip away like melting ice. Jude talked and talked and talked. Laura continued to eat and Jude's lips suddenly became larger than life and all Laura could see was them moving up and down.

"So what do you think?" asked Jude.

Laura stopped looking at Jude's lips and realised she had no idea what her date had been saying.

"Well...I... um...it's all relative," she responded, with what she hoped would be a non-committal answer.

Jude starred at Laura intensely. "I suppose so. My ex was amazing," continued Jude, and explained to Laura why.

Oh my God, thought Laura in resignation, I am so bored. I am on a date with this hot woman and she is boring the pants off me. How can I get away? I will say I have an appointment with my therapist. Maybe that might put her off.

"...and the way her eyes twinkled, it was like looking at the stars at night..."

I am definitely NOT ordering dessert, Laura thought, even though the banoffee pie looks amazing.

"...you know, love like that doesn't come around twice..."

Can I repeat the 'I need the toilet' trick? Laura's mind continued to race. She looked around her and saw the ladies toilets were in direct view of their table. Damn! Maybe I can get someone to call me? she thought desperately. Yes, that's what I'll do.

"...all our friends thought we would get married..."

"Just tragic," agreed Laura, shaking her head. "Sorry but I just need to pop to the ladies, then I will be right back."

"No problem, Lisa," said Jude.

"It's Laura," said Laura to an unhearing Jude.

"By the way, you have ketchup on your face," Jude pointed out.

Laura touched her face and felt a splodge of tomato sauce on her cheek. She hurried to the bathroom.

"..and in five minutes, call me and hang up." Laura spoke on her phone to Jane, as she used a tissue to clean her cheek. "No, I don't have time to explain, just trust me, ok?"

Laura sat back down and saw that Jude had eaten the rest of her burger. "Dessert?" Jude asked as she waved the waiter over.

"That would be lovely," lied Laura.

Laura looked at the menu as Jude began talking again. "...and when we went to the Maldives, I thought I had died and gone to heaven and she was my angel..."

Ring! Ring!

Laura took her phone out of her bag, and looking at it said, "Sorry, I have to take this, it's my mum."

"Hi Mum," said Laura.

"Mum?" said Jane on the other end. "Now I don't think I look old enough! Maybe I do need that botox after all."

"Really? That's awful," continued Laura. "When did this happen?"

"Laura, are you on a date again? Look, stay safe, ok?" Jane hung up.

"Oh dear, I know, I will come over straight away." Laura mouthed sorry at Jude. "Look, keep calm and I can be with you in fifteen minutes. Yes. Yes. I love you too."

Laura put her phone in her bag. She made her excuses and left.

It was the end of another school year and Laura was in her classroom, putting some files into a box, as she prepared to leave school and enjoy the summer holidays.

"What are your plans for the summer?" asked Jane as they both walked to their cars. "Richard and I are going to spend a few days in Menorca, and then we have family coming to stay."

"You know, the usual - relaxing, catching up with friends," replied Laura. Getting 15 cats and becoming the archetypal crazy lady! she thought to herself.

"Well, have a good one," waved Jane, reversing her car out of the car park. "Keep in touch and we'll meet up for a drink."

Laura scrolled down the list of GaydarGirls in her area. She looked at a profile. No. Another one. No. Another one. Oh come on! she thought, this one definitely has to be a bored housewife.

Ping! A message appeared in her inbox. Laura read it.

'Hi Cinderella, my name is Maria. Great profile.'

Laura, feeling a polite sense of duty, typed back, 'Thanks.'

'I am in your area this week and wondered if you wanted to meet.'

Laura sighed. I just can't go on another disastrous date. *'Sorry but I am away this week. Maybe another time.'*

'No problem. Just thought it would be nice to meet up with someone local. Here's my mobile, if you are around when I next visit. You can call, so you know I am who I say I am. I am genuine. Have a good evening.'

It was the middle of August and Laura was at a country manor, celebrating her brother's wedding. She sat at a table, watching her brother and his new wife dancing happily, whilst the dance floor began to get crowded. Laura drank her Champagne. She was so happy for her brother. That's what I want, she thought. Someone to love and who loves me. It's not asking for the world, is it?

Laura took her phone out of her bag and connected to the internet. She looked at her Facebook page, then saw another window was still open: GaydarGirls. She clicked on it and re-read Maria's message, noticing she still had Maria's number. Laura watched other couples dancing and avoided making eye-contact with her brother's male friend, drunkenly smiling inanely at her, from across the dance floor. Oh why not? Laura thought, the Champagne fuzzing her senses. What do I have to lose? Her conscience answered her - your self-respect, your dignity. Laura, you need to be careful, you don't want to get your heart broken again, do you? Laura waved it away and called Maria's number.

"Si?" A Spanish woman answered the phone.

"Oh, I think I have the wrong number. Is that Maria?" asked Laura.

"Yes," came the reply. "Who is this?"

"I'm Cinderella82, from GaydarGirls," said Laura, her confidence bolstered by the Champagne. "You gave me your number."

"Ah si, I remember," said Maria.

"You said to call if I was around and well...if you are ever in the area again, it would be nice to meet up," Laura finished quickly, her heart thudding.

"Sure. I will be around next week," replied Maria.

Laura waited nervously outside the Sacre Bleu French restaurant. She had texted Maria a couple of times and they had spoken on the phone, and so far, she had not found anything that rang alarm bells. She had learnt that Maria was Spanish and worked for a hotel chain, based in Barcelona. Her job meant frequent travelling and she often came to the UK.

They had arranged to meet at 8 o'clock. Laura looked at her watch. It was 8.10. Great, she thought, she isn't going to turn up. Suddenly she heard a voice call her name.

"Hola, Laura."

Laura looked up as Maria walked towards her. She had short, dark hair and was wearing skinny black jeans, black shoes, a blue shirt and a dark leather jacket. So far, so good, thought Laura, with a little trepidation.

Maria kissed Laura on both cheeks.

"You look lovely, guapa," she said.

"Thanks. You too," replied Laura honestly.

Laura had made an effort for her date, despite her previous experiences, and had opted for a black lacy top, dark blue jeans and black high heel shoes.

"Shall we?" smiled Maria as she held the door of the restaurant open for Laura.

As Laura looked through the menu, she said, "Do you know, I didn't even realise this town had a French restaurant!"

Maria laughed and looked into her eyes, "You are funny."

"No, I am serious," said Laura.

Maria continued to laugh as she read the menu.

Laura looked over the top of her menu and noticed how deep and dark Maria's eyes were, with the most amazing long lashes. Laura was momentarily mesmerised. She continued to look into her eyes before mentally kicking herself, returning her attention to the wine section. Laura felt Maria's eyes on her, as if she were silently appraising her.

As the evening progressed, Laura felt herself relax with Maria, and they talked to each other with ease, getting to know each other, and found they shared the same sense of humour. When the bill came, Laura reached down for her purse. Maria put her hand over Laura's. "Guapa, you are my guest. I couldn't possibly let you," and she gave her credit card to the waiter.

Leaving the restaurant, Laura spoke. "Thank you for dinner, it was lovely. And your company, of course," she quickly added.

Maria smiled. "You are welcome and thank you for your company. I have had a lovely evening with you."

They both stood outside of the restaurant. Laura thought desperately for something interesting or witty to say, but in her state of nervous excitement, she was rendered speechless; tumbleweed blowing through her brain. Luckily, Maria broke the silence.

"I have to fly back to Barcelona tomorrow morning, but I would really like to see you again. I will be back in the UK next week. Maybe we could spend some more time together?"

Laura's heart skipped a beat, and she found her voice. "Yes I would really like that. That would be lovely."

"Unfortunately, I need to get back to my hotel now; my flight is very early," said Maria, "but I will call you."

She looked intently into Laura's eyes and moved closer to her. Laura stood, frozen to the spot. Her heart was thudding so fast, she was sure Maria could see it pumping through her chest.

Maria bent down and gently brushed her lips against Laura's. Laura closed her eyes and kissed her back, breathing in the scent of her perfume.

Maria broke the kiss as a taxi pulled up. She stroked Laura's cheek and Laura opened her eyes.

"Until next time," Maria said and got into the taxi. "Hasta luego."

Laura lifted her hand and waved as Maria left in the taxi, then touched her lips with her fingers, where a millisecond earlier, Maria's lips had been. She remembered to breathe again.

Laura watched as the taxi disappeared from view, then she searched in her bag for her phone. She called Jane's number.

Jane answered sleepily, "Hey sweetheart, are you ok?"

"I am more than ok," answered Laura.

"What?" Jane was confused, still half-asleep.

"I am great!" replied Laura laughing, picturing the story of Cinderella in her mind. "I think I am about to have my own fairytale," she continued happily.

###

DEBORAH UNDERWOOD is a primary school teacher, who lives happily in sunny Spain with her partner of seven years. Contrary to popular belief, they have neither cats nor children. Deborah loves to read and as a child her favourite story was Cinderella, especially the part when Cinders is all dressed up for the Prince's ball. That really should have been a sign. *Looking for Princess Charming* is Deborah's first, and possibly last, foray into the world of lesbian chick lit.

CLOUD HEARTS
Angela Peach

I WASN'T SURE that Elizabeth was going to turn up, but I was nervously waiting anyway. This *was* where we'd arranged to meet, but we hadn't exactly parted on good terms. That was quite possibly the understatement of the century. She'd screamed and begged for me to stay, but in the end I'd had to turn my back on her and walk away, squeezing my eyes shut so I wouldn't feel tempted for one last look. I'd succeeded, but it had left a bitter ache in my soul. For years I'd regretted not getting that last look.

So here I was, waiting and hoping beyond hope that she'd found the strength to forgive. Forgive herself for…well, for what she'd done, and forgive me for leaving her. This was the meadow where we'd known, simultaneously, that we were in love, the realization hitting us both as we lay watching the clouds. I knew if I were to close my eyes I could remember it as if it was yesterday, but I don't because I want to see her when she arrives.

If she arrives.

My breathing quickens with anxiety. Surely she would come? I fidget, picking a stone out of the dusty ground and throwing it into the grass as I try to remind myself just how unpredictable my Elizabeth had been. It was one of the many things I'd loved about her, how she'd always kept me on my toes, never failing to make me laugh out loud.

She'd never been stunning to look at, but had possessed an incredible inner beauty that shone out from within, and it was that which captivated you, that got your attention and made you look closer as you tried to work out what it'd been that had drawn your eye in the first place. Her lips were thin, but would stretch into the widest, most engaging smile with ease. Behind her glasses were big clear eyes that could fluctuate between an intense jade green to a calm azure blue, flecked with gold, and when they focused on you, you felt like the most important person in the world. (Well, that's how I always felt anyway.) Her hair changed colour too, but that was down to whatever took her fancy more than anything else. It wasn't unusual for me to come home to find I was living with a punk or a redhead or some other extreme.

And I'd loved her. Whatever colour hair she'd had, or eyes even, I'd just loved her for being her. I'd especially loved her for being mine.

I smile, thinking back to the day we'd met. I'd just popped into a shop for some cigarettes (a disgusting habit that I'd quit a couple of weeks later with El's help) and as I'd walked out of the shop in a hurry I'd bumped into her. Quite literally. We'd both mumbled apologies (while I discreetly scrutinised her unusual eyes) before she walked off, leaving me watching her in kind of a state of shock. Something about her felt so familiar, so...so...?

It was as I was struggling to think of the word that she turned and looked over her shoulder at me, a curious smile on her face. Caught out staring, I raised my hand to wave, not knowing what else to do. Neither of us saw the lamp-post in her path until it was too late. There was an audible crack as she ricocheted backwards, falling onto her arse and rolling so her legs and feet almost came over her head. She stayed where she was, rubbing her head and staring up at the obstruction with an extremely perplexed expression. Slapping a hand over my mouth to suppress the giggle that was bubbling up, I rushed to her aid.

"Hey, are you all right?" I asked, my voice shaking with the effort of containing my hysteria. She turned to look at me, her face a comical display of dazed confusion and surprise, and it literally took everything I had to keep mine straight. She frowned (which, she'd later explained, was because she was trying to focus – luckily she hadn't been wearing her glasses when she'd walked into the post) and then suddenly dissolved into hysterical laughter. I saw this as a great big glowing neon green light to let mine loose, and within seconds I was crouched on the ground next to her, holding her arm for support. Because, you see, even back then when we were complete strangers, we still felt like old friends.

Comfortable. That was the word I'd been searching for.

Just as my laughter started to subside, she re-enacted the boing from the post, throwing her legs in the air, and we both started cackling again like hyenas on laughing gas. We didn't care that we might look slightly crazy hunched on the pavement with tears running down our cheeks. This was our moment, and it was the first of many.

"What's your name?" she finally managed, her eyes focusing on mine and creating an odd curious falling sensation inside me. I held out my hand.

"Pippa. And yours?"

"Elizabeth. Well Pippa, it truly is a pleasure to meet you."

"Likewise. How's your head?"

"How's my...? Oh! Yes, my head's fine. Wish I could say the same about my pride."

We both stood up before awkwardly shuffling our feet, reluctant to just walk away from each other and bring our encounter to an end. I cleared my throat.

"Would you like to join me for a drink?" I blurted, and she nodded enthusiastically.

"Sure. That'd be nice."

I decided my mother and sister wouldn't mind my being a little late for the wedding dress fitting (and they mightn't have, except a little late turned into a lot late!) And as El and I had parted that day, we'd swapped numbers, eagerly promising to meet again soon.

That had been the beginning, and where are we now? Hopefully not the end? Hopefully a *new* beginning.

I scan the meadow again, looking to see if there are any secret entrances I don't know about where she could sneak up on me by surprise, but I already know there's only the one way in.

Come on Elizabeth? Please?

Today is a perfect replica of the day we'd found this place. I think back, to the blue skies, deep and rich with a scattering of cute, fluffy white clouds being gently urged on by a warm summer's breeze.

(And not those off grey ones either – these were pure white, resembling handfuls of cotton wool scattered happily in the sky.) The long grass that had swished gently to and fro around the small private area we'd flattened to lie back in hiding us from the world, and the rest of the world from us.

But it'd been a relatively slow build up to that point, with us spending the first month just meeting for drinks and lunches here and there. The second found us spending whole days together whenever we could, interspersed with lengthy night-time phone conversations. As the third month rolled around, I remembered I had a plus one to my sister's wedding and very shyly invited El. She very shyly accepted.

Ah. The wedding. The day I realised my feelings ran so much deeper than mere friendship (and, as was always the case with us, when she had the same mind blowing revelation). I hadn't been able to take my eyes off her the whole day. In fact, I couldn't tell you a single detail about my sister's wedding dress, but I could tell you that El had been wearing a simple long vision of cream satin that hugged her body from slender shoulders to her bare legs, teasing out every now and then through a tasteful slit that stopped just above her knee. She'd chosen to dye her hair a rich chestnut brown, with highlights woven through that gave her an air of sophistication. I'd never seen her look, nor act so elegantly before, and I proudly paraded her by my side the entire day, each of us totally engrossed by the other and ignoring all offers of drinks and dances that came our way. My dad kept winking at us and saying things like "It'll be you next." I'd just assumed he meant me, but he hadn't. He'd meant *us*; it'd be *us* next.

Elizabeth had known exactly what he meant and it was she who mentioned it to me later that evening as we drunkenly helped each other out of our dresses. I'd stared at her stood before me in just her underwear, her beautiful aqua green eyes meeting mine uncertainly as she waited for my response. But I couldn't answer. I was suddenly overcome with the urge to continue undressing her, for my fingertips to caress her skin as the dress had. To love her.

While I was being shaken by these thoughts, she mistook my silence for disagreement and ran to the bathroom, leaving me to try and find some air for my useless lungs.

I tried to put it all down to the high running emotions of the day teamed with excessive alcohol, but when I woke the next morning, one look at her in the other bed was all it took. I knew I wanted more. I wanted it all. But I was so scared of losing our beautiful friendship I kept my thoughts and feelings to myself.

Again, as did she.

Who knows how long we might've skirted round it, had not my father suffered a fatal heart attack only three weeks after the wedding. I'd called El straight away, sobbing down the phone at her, and she was at my door within minutes it seemed, where I'd fallen into her helplessly. She held me tight, trying to absorb my pain and replace it with her love. I lost myself in that embrace for a while, holding her as if she'd dissolve should I relinquish my grip.

When finally we drew back, I saw she'd been crying too. She traced my tears from my cheeks with soft fingertips, her eyes full of pain and love.

"Come on. Let's go for a walk and get some air, eh?"

She put some snacks and drinks into a rucksack while I got dressed, then we headed for the woods just outside of town where we knew it would be peaceful and far from people. As we walked, El took my hand in her own, smiling warmly. It was enough to make my breath catch in my throat.

"I think I need a cigarette," I whispered, more from the shock of tingles blossoming from her touch than because of grief. She'd laughed nervously.

"Me too, but if I can resist, so can you."

As I looked sideways at her, she winked quickly, causing my heart to riot against my rib cage.

We walked in silence for a while, both comfortable enough not to feel the need to fill it unnecessarily. I was both psyching myself up for and dreading the long journey to Mum and...well, Mum's house. Almost as if reading my mind, El gave my hand a gentle squeeze.

"Pippa? If you want some company when you go, I'd be happy to come with you. Unless of course it's just a family thing, then I..."

"No! I mean, yes. I mean I'd really like it if you came with me. But only if you're sure you don't mind?"

"Of course not, I just wish I could do more for you. I hate seeing you like this. I know I only met him once, but I really liked him. He seemed like a good man."

"Yes. He was."

She paused.

"He...he asked me to look after you. Made me promise to, actually."

I stopped walking and stared at her in shock, unable to say anything. She studied me closely as she said, "I promised him that I would. Because I love you."

"Thank you," I whispered, her words like a warm glove around my pain. She seemed satisfied with my reaction and we continued our walk, our bodies closer together. We didn't have a destination in mind, and it was probably how we stumbled accidentally onto the meadow.

"I had no idea this was here," I gasped, leaning into her.

"Me neither. It's just beautiful!"

We stepped through the knee-high grass until we reached the centre and then Elizabeth suddenly threw herself down on the ground, rolling around on it until she'd flattened an area big enough for us both to lie down. She looked up at me and patted the ground next to her, her eyes compassionate and watching me closely as I lowered myself down.

"Pip? If you want to have a cry, or talk about your dad, or just lie here quietly, you just go ahead. Whatever you want, it's ok."

And that's exactly what I did. As the day passed I recounted random memories from my childhood with my head in the crook of her shoulder. After my telling her his favourite song was Jeff Buckley's version of *Hallelujah*, she'd sung it quietly to me and I'd buried my tears in her chest. But mostly we just watched those fluffy clouds pass us by.

"Pippa, close your eyes! Close them!" She placed her hands over them anyway, even as I complied. "Ok, now think about your dad. Ask him for a sign, just for you."

I did as she asked and she gently removed her hands, speaking in a breathless whisper.

"Open your eyes and look up."

My eyelids fluttered open and I gasped. Directly above us was a perfect heart-shaped cloud. A lump formed in my throat as we both watched it, caught up in the magic of the moment. But what happened next, three things in a row, was even more magical.

The first was a beam of light hitting the heart at such an angle it gave it the appearance of glowing brightly, setting it apart from all the other clouds. The second was a perfectly timed hawk that soared across our vision and hovered for a few perfect seconds in the heart before falling gracefully away and out of sight.

But the third? I'd turned to Elizabeth to say something about the hawk and heart, and she'd turned to me at the same time. In that split second, my heart stopped beating, my lungs stopped breathing and the world stopped spinning. Time stood still, immortalising us in the moment. I knew we were feeling the same thing as our souls and energies merged because I could see it in her eyes, feel it pulsing between us in powerful waves. I thought my heart might swell and float away with the cloud heart.

We lay like that for a while, just gazing at each other as if for the first time, knowing we were in love and allowing the emotion to consume us like fire. I'm not sure how long it was before our lips got tired of waiting and joined together for their own union, but that was when the world around us dissolved away. Tentative and soft at first, we took our time exploring each other. We had time and eternity on our side, after all. We made love with a tender passion, and although neither of us came, we were utterly content with the pleasures experienced.

Later that afternoon we'd dressed and returned to my flat. Despite the crushing grief of losing Dad and knowing what was ahead, my spirit was soaring thanks to El and the heart and the hawk. I truly felt everything was going to be ok, so long as we had each other.

Oh Elizabeth, I hope you realise this is our last chance to be together? If you don't turn up today, we'll never see each other again.

The thought brings me crashing out of my daydream and back to earth like a block of cement as my anxiety deepens, because it's true. If she fails to show today I'll know for certain that she'd been unable to forgive herself for what she'd done, even if it meant losing me forever.

I never once blamed you, my love. Please, let go of the past and come back to me.

I wish desperately that I could go to her, tell her it wasn't her fault and show her that we could still have a future together. But I don't know where she is so I *have* to wait here, because this is the time and place we'd arranged to meet. Has she forgiven me, I wonder, for leaving her?

That day. The dark day when I'd realised our forever wasn't as long as I'd imagined. I'd had no choice. I'd *had* to leave, even if it had meant tearing my soul apart leaving my love, my world, my life behind to start anew.

But it's getting late now. I can feel the icy grip of panic in my heart as I realise I've never given any thought to what I might do if she doesn't come. I'd always just assumed she would.

And as the sun starts to set, it brings a cold darkness to the meadow, *our* meadow, that spreads into my soul. I sink to my knees in our spot, crying out in anguish, calling out her name over and over as I clutch my chest, my heart imploding like a black hole, sucking everything in mercilessly.

"Pippa?"

The voice behind me speaks so softly, so uncertainly, I almost dismiss it as a dream, a fantasy. But when I feel a hand on my shoulder, the sun explodes back into the sky, the fluffy clouds return and my heart starts beating again!

"El? Elizabeth? Oh my god, you remembered! You came!" I jump to my feet, throwing my arms around her with such force we both crash to the ground in a heap. I laugh as I bestow kisses on her, my tears mixing with her own. At first she resists, demanding to know what's going on. But it's not too long before she accepts my mouth with hers, hungrily bruising together. We make love under the clouds, both laughing and crying with pure joy. (And this time we both come.)

"Pippa, is it really you? Are you really here?" she asks, trembling fingers tracing the contours of my face.

"Yes, I'm really here. *You're* really here!"

"I don't understand what's happening?"

"It doesn't matter, baby. What matters is that I waited for you and you came."

"Oh god, I hated myself so much. It...it ate me up inside. There were so many times I thought about ending it all, just to escape the pain." She sees me wince and kisses me. "I never wanted to hurt you. I would have given my life a thousand times over for you, a billion times even. Because I didn't just hurt you, Pippa, I didn't *just* cause you pain..."

"It's ok. It's ok," I soothe, knowing it's important that we both face this now so we can truly move on.

"It's not ok. It was *never* ok. I killed you! I killed you!"

"El, it wasn't your fault. It was an accident, just a terrible accident." I take her hands and make her aqua-marine eyes meet mine so she can see I'm sincere. "I never blamed you. I only ever loved you."

The scenery around us shifts and changes, transporting us back to an overcast day in Thailand. We'd gone there on our seven year anniversary, travelling around the beautiful islands for seven weeks – one for each year.

We'd only managed twenty eight days.

Detached from this reality we both watch as our younger selves approach a young lad selling soup and noodles, as El playfully insists to me that she knows enough of the language and orders in Thai. As we chat about our plans for the next few days while eating the bowls of food, I feel Present-El grip my hand tightly as my past-self frowns and coughs, touching a hand to her throat and rasping, "Honey, I can't breathe...are you sure there's no shellfish in this?"

I want to close my eyes, but I force myself to watch, hoping Elizabeth is too. This will be our closure so we can both move on.

Past-El suddenly drops her bowl and starts screaming for a doctor as she rushes to help, while Past-Me clutches at my constricting airways. (I wasn't sure what had been worse. My inability to breathe, or the panic and pain on Elizabeth's face.) Helpless to do anything, she screams at me.

"Don't you *dare*, Pippa, don't you dare leave me? You stay with me baby, you're strong, just please don't die, don't leave me, please, *please*, PLEASE?"

I listen to her words, remembering how they'd cut into my soul as I'd slipped further and further away from her. Because even after I'd separated from my body, I could still hear her begging and pleading with me not to leave her. But I'd had no choice.

Watching her heart break again in front of me is no less painful second time around, more so in fact. I turn to Present-El beside me.

"Baby, you have to let go of the past. We have to let go of it *together*."

"But...does that mean...am I dead? This isn't just another dream where I wake up and you're gone?"

I remember how the transition between life and death can be very confusing and dreamlike.

"No, you're never going to lose me again. We can start forever properly now." I cup her face softly. "You had cancer. You died a short while ago."

Her eyes widen in shock.

"I remember! Oh Pippa, I remember!" she gasps, and I pull her close to me. It's a shock to the ethereal system when it all floods back and you realise you're not just asleep, that your death was real. I hold her as she sobs it out, feeling tears fall from my own eyes. When she finally pulls back, I brush her hair from her wet cheeks as she admits, "I nearly went the other way. Oh my god, I almost...there was a choice? So hard to remember now..." She squeezes her eyes shut.

"Yes. The other way was if you'd chosen to remain locked in your pain, to punish yourself with your guilt. If you hadn't forgiven yourself you would have gone that way and we'd never have seen each other again. I was so scared, not knowing if you'd be able to release yourself from the past or not."

"I almost didn't. But I remembered here, our promise to wait in the meadow for each other if anything happened to us, and I wondered. If there was the slightest possibility you'd be here, I had to come."

"Yes! That was what made me choose this way. I felt so guilty at leaving you in your pain, for *being* the cause of your pain, I almost went the other way too," I whisper, aware that we've returned to our meadow again. She throws her arms around me and we hold each other tightly for a long time.

"What happens now?" she finally asks, and I smile secretly before pulling back enough to cover her eyes with my hands.

"Close your eyes." When I feel her lashes graze my palms, I move around so I'm stood behind her, resting my head on her shoulder and wrapping my arms around her waist. "Now open them."

Elizabeth opens her eyes and I watch her expression change to one of wondrous awe and delight.

"Pippa? How did you...? Oh my god!"

Above us are thousands of different sized clouds, in every colour of the rainbow...and all of them are perfect hearts, bouncing against each other gently in the vast expanse of sky. She laughs, spinning around with her head thrown back and arms outstretched.

"How did you do this?"

"I've had a long time to practice. Do you like them?"

"Like them? I LOVE THEM!"

I laugh with her, joy and love exploding out of my heart that she's actually here with me. Then I take her hand.

"You asked what happens now. Anything happens now!"

"*Any*thing?"

"*Any*thing! Whatever you want."

Her jade green eyes flicker blue as possibilities flash through her mind. I'm beside myself with excitement for the adventures we are about to embark on, as the time I've spent waiting for her has been just that – waiting for her. She bites her lip.

"Ok, well to start with...I think I want to jump on every single cloud up there like trampolines," she says excitedly. "And I want wings to fly up to them!"

I kiss her softly.

"Then let's go."

###

ANGELA PEACH lives deep in the beautiful New Forest and, when not writing, enjoys meditating, walking her crazy dog and living life to the fullest. Her first novel, *47*, was taken on by Shadoe Publishers and is currently being translated into a screenplay. *The Blurring* was her second novel and went straight to Number 1 on the Amazon lesbian fiction chart, followed quickly by *In Reflection*. But in November 2013 Peach released *Playing My Love* and was totally unprepared for the runaway success as it stormed the charts, going to Number 1 in four different countries and becoming a worldwide bestseller. She's spent the last few months putting together this anthology, but can now go back to work on typing up her next novel, *The L Factor*.

FEELS LIKE HOME
Sarah Bolger

SHIVERING AND yawning in chorus after a day spent marking substandard undergraduate drivel, I strode stiffly out of the Arts Block of Trinity College to the cobblestoned walkways. Making my way to where I had chained up my bike at the back of the building, I donned my luminous cycle vest and velcroed it firmly across my chest. I tucked my right trouser leg into my boot sock and set off, wheeling my ancient, creaking bike across the shadows of the Campanile towards the front arch of the college. As I passed through the gates onto College Green, I was, as ever, exhilarated by the raucous cacophony of boisterous home-time sounds that always engulfed the evening city.

I weaved through the lines of rush-hour traffic and pedalled confidently towards O'Connell Bridge. The light mist of November rain developed into a downpour as I waited at the traffic lights to cross over the bridge. Enormous, heavy drops plastered my short blond hair to my forehead and rivulets of water flowed down my face into my eyes, blurring my view of the Ha'penny Footbridge west along the River Liffey. It was 5.40pm and I knew that my best friend and flatmate, Fionnuala, would be sitting impatiently at the bar in Mayes pub waiting for me, unmoved by my oft-used explanations for tardiness. Efficiently clocking out of her supervisor's job at Clerys Department Store on the button at 5pm daily Monday to Friday, she had little empathy for my underpaid, overworked position as TA in Trinity's English faculty. That's not to say that she hadn't been my rock through six years of study and self-doubt.

After weaving three heavy-duty chains around my bike and some rusted railings, I began ripping open my high-viz jacket and pushed open the pub door to be greeted by the pungent, familiar and oddly comforting aroma of spilled stout, Joxer's pipe smoke and John Player Blue cigarettes – not to mention stinky old man Guinness farts: familiar territory.

"Ha, Jacinta, sight for sore eyes you are! Enjoy yer swim?" This was Ray, the barman, our little ray of sunshine; ever the gentleman... or not.

"Feck off, Ray, and how many times do I have to tell ye. Even my ma doesn't call me Jacinta anymore. Stick with Jay, will ye?"

"Right you are, *Jacinta*." He winked cheekily and tipped his imaginary cap in my direction. "Pint, is it?"

"Please."

I searched the length of the bar for Fionnuala's familiarly unruly auburn curls. I spotted her sitting in a snug in the far corner of the pub, scrutinising a magazine in front of her with an enigmatic smile on her face.

"Oi, slapper, how's tricks? Escape from the land of knickers early today, then?" I raised my voice and winked impertinently at her across the bar. Fionnuala's supervisory position was in the lingerie department at the store.

Her reverie broken, she looked up and registered my presence with a slow grin that spread rapidly to her hazel eyes. I wondered what had her looking so thrilled. "Mine's a gin and tonic," she yelled across, mightily disturbing two disgruntled old gents sitting in the next alcove, heads together over the racing forms in the Evening Herald.

Ray jerked his head towards our seat, signalling that he would bring our drinks over. I smiled my thanks and squelched over to Fionnuala. I grabbed a small stool and plonked myself down on it with a contented sigh. Being here with Fionnuala, away from books and study, basking in her fun affection, always warmed me. Fionnuala put her hand on my forearm and drew my attention to the magazine in front of her.

"Get a load of this, Jay!"

Fionnuala manically brandished the latest "hot off the press" issue of *Hot Press* in my face, narrowly avoiding taking my eye out with its corner. She was always one for getting in a tizzy over what she perceived to be the "controversial issues of our changing times". I mindlessly wondered what had gotten her goat this time; we'd already done abortion and divorce that week, with some of Fionnuala's best ever stand-alone sound-bites the product of those discussions. Colourful had probably always been the best word to describe our Fionnuala's mode of communication. Blunt might be another. I braced myself.

"Well, hand it over then, so I can see what you're goin' on about." Fionnuala again gesticulated crazily with her index finger at the photograph on the front page, obviously used to show just how willingly controversial and "with it" the editors considered themselves to be. It was, after all, 1999, and we were in "good auld Catholic Ireland". I glanced nonchalantly at the image at first, until I absorbed with horror what I was looking at. An army of butterflies flapped their way through my innards as I broke out all over in a nervous sweat. I looked again and double-took. It needed yet another look. Fuck. Shit.

Proud as you like, two topless women, boobs a-dangling, strode along the centre of O'Connell Street, Dublin's main thoroughfare. Their arms were draped casually around each other as they marched, hip to hip and engaged in a no-holds-barred, tongue-twisting snog to end all snogs. Obviously engineered for the cameras and for the viewing horror of Ireland's ultra-conservative Catholic patriarchy, I knew this would be an iconic image to go down in the annals of Irish political history. This was Dublin's gay pride parade, from just the weekend before.

However, it wasn't the lustful ladies that had me all a-flutter and on the verge of panic; just left of centre and over the shoulders supporting one delectable pair of boobs, an all-too-familiar face peeked in the direction of the photo's subjects: me.

In the nanosecond before it took Fionnuala to clock my reaction, a gazillion thoughts speared my mind: 'I tried to say no'; 'What'll I tell my Ma?' With absolutely no trace of irony, I realised this sounded like my own self-admonitions following the loss of my teenage virginity to Anto Doyle out the back of the flats where I grew up. Déjà vu!

Fionnuala stared at me curiously; she'd known me almost as long as I'd known myself, having misspent her youth around at my ma's flat when escaping the blazing drunken rows between her dysfunctional parents in their flat two floors below. Although my da took off when I was born (apparently he didn't deal well with the realities of parenthood), my ma had been my backbone through a plethora of childhood and teenage traumas. In spite of growing up during one of the blackest periods of economic depression in Irish history, I was always well-fed, warm and loved. By default, so was Fionnuala. We did all the clichéd 'firsts' together, apart from sex of course, although she did talk me into playing look-out around the dustbins while she completed her own rite-of-passage mission of seducing Jamie Foxton and taking her first steps to womanhood.

"Are ye all right, Jay?" she asked me quietly, ducking her head to force me to meet her eyes.

"Yeh, I'm grand, sure. Just came over all dizzy, that's all." I stared down at the table top and picked at my fingernails. After about half an awkward minute, I glanced warily up and met her eyes again. I wasn't surprised to see that they were full of mirthful mischief and something resembling gleeful triumph.

"Mmm-hmm, and that has nothin' to do with the blatant fact that your ugly mug is staring right back at us from behind those lovely lezzers, eh?" Grinning, she waited for my much delayed full reaction. She broke into excited laughter.

"Come on, Jay, out with it!" By this point, she was almost delirious with the hilarity of her own joke. "Get it? 'OUT' with it?" She collapsed into a fit of thrilled giggles and I glared at her in shock, rapidly attempting to regain some semblance of control over this nightmare-scenario-turned-reality. I struggled to find the words.

"Just what exactly are you insinuating, Fionnuala? That I am some kind of muff-buffer like that dirty pair?" I pretended outrage, respectively stabbing a finger at the photo and then in her face. She was having none of it.

"I was there to support a friend, that's all," I finished lamely. What I desperately didn't want Fionnuala to know was that this so-called friend was my posh, Dalkey-dwelling girlfriend-of-a-sort, in action if not in name, Síofra Dooley, daughter of millionaire property tycoon, Damien Dooley of Dooley Enterprises Inc. If it was possible, Síofra was even more deeply ensconced in that proverbial closet than I was, in spite of my new Navratilova 'do and Doc Marten sixteen-holes. Síofra, at least, seemed to believe I cut quite the figure, even if I did hail from the dirt-poor 'Northside' of Dublin, in contrast with her privileged 'Southside' Dalkey environs and lifestyle.

Fionnuala daggered one mocking eyebrow in my direction. She recognised my knee-jerk defensives a mile off, just like I was well-acquainted with every irrational foible, fear and emotion of hers, much discussed and psychoanalysed over late-night cans of Dutch Gold in the tiny living room of our shared one-bed in Nelson Street.

"Well fuck me pink and purple, Jacinta O'Donovan. I've known about your latent homosexuality for years, but this internalised self-hating homophobia is a new one on me." As I said: colourful. She clasped her hands in front of her, flexing her fingers in a mockery of the professional manner of some upmarket, over-paid psychiatrist. "So tell me, Miss O'Donovan, how long have you been suffering from these deep-seated delusions of heterosexuality?" Her tone was that of a female Sigmund Freud, even down to the terrible Germanic accent that made her sound like a poorly-acted Nazi from a 1960s Steve McQueen movie.

I glared at her in exasperation but couldn't maintain it. Fionnuala knew me too bloody well. I sighed worriedly and looked up at her, feeling vulnerable as hell.

"Well? Come *on* Jay, I've known ever since I caught ye staring at that Miss Kelly's arse in English class back in first year, right before she pegged the board duster at you for not paying proper attention." Fionnuala winked ostentatiously. "I think she was flirting with ye!"

I huffed. "Oh, fuck off, you win." My shoulders slumped and I could feel the tears of frustration clouding my vision. What happened next almost made me fall off my chair, sloshing half of my pint of Guinness all over the table, much to Ray's chagrin.

Fionnuala leapt up out of her chair, whooping deafeningly at the top of her lungs.

"Well, Halle-freakin'-lujah! YEARS, I've been waiting for this moment. Barkeep," Fionnuala bellowed, "a bottle of yer finest! We have some celebrating to do." She dug deep into her pockets and pulled out a handful of pound coins, but no notes. "Um, on second thoughts, Ray, a bottle of Blue Nun will have to do." She looked at me apologetically. "Assistant Department Floor Supervisor for Lingerie in Clerys doesn't quite stretch that far. Sorry." I could only chuckle. As far as accidental 'outings' go, this hadn't been the worst, not by a long shot.

Queuing up outside the Temple Bar Music Centre was the most diverse mix of females to gather in one place since Woodstock: from punks to grungers, butch to femme, dresses to jeans, smiling to scowling... I had only been to this event once before – this was "Kiss", Dublin's only monthly lesbian night.

In true Dublin style, Temple Bar's cobbles were wet and slippery from the consistent November rain that could chill you to the core in seconds. I had decided that my retro X-Worx jeans, loosely hanging around my hips and bum, with a green tank top and black hoodie would suffice as my evening's uniform. The requisite Doc boots were always worn at this time of year, but I'd decided that my bottle-green eight-holes would better suit my newly buoyant mood this evening. Since my coerced outing to Fionnuala the previous week, she had been not only accepting of the status quo but downright exuberant about it. This merely served to make me chuckle and ask myself for the umpteenth time why I hadn't confided in her years earlier. One thing was for sure: there would be no more secrets between me and the woman I was closest to in the whole world – the woman who in full, supportive best-friend, warrior mode, had insisted on accompanying me to Temple Bar for this event and to meet the fabled Síofra.

Hence the grumbling, whinging best friend I was gallantly escorting by the arm across the slippery cobbles to the front entrance. I had to admit, I had always admired and been a tad envious of Fionnuala's ability to transform the most basic, seemingly mismatched items of clothing into an ensemble that not only worked but made her even more charismatic and attractive than her toned curves, bouncy shoulder-length curls and impish hazel eyes already achieved. There had been a time during our teenage years when I genuinely thought the sun shone out of her arse; I proactively put that little crush away after a couple of painful years of unrequited love. Then I headed off to college and the world of available women opened up before me through Trinity's new LGB society.

"Ah, the curse of hell on it! Why, oh, why did I think that these heels were a good idea?" Fionnuala pleaded with her eyes and I grabbed hold of her around the waist again, steering her towards the door of the venue. "And as for mascara, is there any left on my eyelashes or is it all now running down my face?" Her frustration and impracticality made me laugh out loud, which in its turn earned me a firm smack across the back of my head.

"Ouch!"

"Serves ye bloody right."

I grinned apologetically. "All ye had to do was take me up on my offer of a pair of docs, ye fool. That would have solved half the problem. And ye would have got here faster out of the rain too."

Fionnuala glanced at me mischievously out of the corner of her eye. "With this dress? Not a bloody chance. And anyway, it's much more fun playing your damsel in distress and having you run around after me. Have you not noticed how much I enjoy your chivalry?" A sassy wink accompanied that last question; Fionnuala's flirtatious nature often threatened to resurrect that decade-old crush with a vengeance.

"So where's this mysterious bird of yours? She here yet?"

"Um, I think you'll find that would be me? And you are?" My heartbeat quickened at the sound of Síofra's voice behind us, but the obvious frost in her voice made me instantly wary. As I gently released Fionnuala's waist, I turned to meet cold, angry blue eyes glaring at me from beneath a coal-black Cleopatra fringe. Uh-oh. I reached for her, smiling, but she backed away, raising her palms to ward me off.

"Jay, I asked a question. Who. Is. She?" She verbally punctuated the question for dramatic effect.

It's funny how certain characteristics can instantly make an individual less attractive. This aggressive jealousy was not new. I attempted to smooth over the situation with that winning Jay-charm that had always worked so well prior to tonight.

I opened my palms wide and magnanimously introduced the pair with a smile that, in that moment, was as wide as my arms. "Síofra, Fionnuala. Finally, the two main ladies in my life meet." I was definitely less smooth than I thought; a scowl from Síofra and an incredulous eyebrow from my best friend told me that my conciliatory tactics were failing miserably.

"Ok, come on you two, start over. Síofra, this is Fionnuala, my best friend since Pampers were our most outrageous fashion statement. I told you all about her over the phone."

Síofra flipped her gaze critically between Fionnuala and me.

"Do you always throw your arms around your best friends and, like, flirt *outrageously*, or is that just the ones that flirt with you first?" she challenged. Crap. She must have been listening for longer than I thought.

"Oh, for crying out loud!" I glanced nervously at Fionnuala, she of the immensely unpredictable temper and big gob; I was actually intrigued to gauge her reaction to Síofra's blatant shit-stirring. To my relief, Fionnuala smiled sweetly, glancing at me placatingly out of the corner of her eye. Taking a step towards Síofra (who visibly recoiled, possibly expecting Fionnuala to stick her forehead on her face), she extended her hand.

"Ah here, look, sorry if it looked like that. It's lovely to meet ya. Sure, we've only been besties since forever."

Wow. This new diplomacy was a revelation. I had never known Fi back down on a challenge, especially from someone she would normally brand a "poshy Southsider" like Síofra. To be honest, before this evening, I hadn't properly noticed myself how nasally snooty Síofra could be. Combined with her hostility, she wasn't measuring up well and I felt a hint of embarrassment.

Síofra sniffed dismissively and imperiously turned to face me. "Jay, it's cold and I'm soaking wet. Take my coat to the cloakroom." She dumped her coat over my arm and began making her way into the club. "Oh, and mine's a white wine. Medium." That was me firmly put in my place. With that, she flounced away to the dance floor. Once she was out of earshot, Fionnuala turned to me, both eyebrows reaching skyward. Uh-oh.

She shook her head disbelievingly, auburn curls bouncing emphatically as if they agreed wholeheartedly with their owner.

"Where the hell did ye find her? Dial-a-bitch? Or is she one of those idiot designer tracksuit kids that hail from the land of "Daddy'll pay for it"?" I squirmed uncomfortably, much to Fionnuala's amusement. She was way too close on this one.

"One more chance, Jay. She has one more chance or I'll cave her smug face in for her first chance I get. I'm sure Daddy could pay for the reconstructive surgery anyway." Her tone became more serious and her smirk faded. "Seriously though, Jay, don't let her talk to you like that. You deserve better. If I..." She stopped there. Her hazel eyes melted as they met mine and she softly repeated "You deserve better." Turning abruptly on her heel and breaking the moment, she called back over her shoulder with a wink: "Mine's a vodka and red bull. Let's get this bloody party started!"

To the dulcet tones of Shaggy's *Oh Carolina*, I drunkenly worked the dance floor with Fionnuala. After handing over a bottle of medium white, I had barely seen Síofra all night. The last time she had staggered over, she'd had some bimbo in a mini-dress on her arm who she drunkenly introduced as her new best friend. "Isn't she really pretty, Jay?" she slurred. I could still see the pair of them bumping and grinding, hot and heavy, on the far side of the dance floor. I was mysteriously unperturbed and, having attempted reconciliation unsuccessfully, I was having a whale of a time swinging my best friend around the dance floor, enjoying the envious looks from other women keen to get a look-in with my bombshell best friend.

In the middle of *Informer* about half an hour later, Síofra stormed over again, eyes blazing. "Here cometh trouble", I thought.

"I should have known fucking better, Jay O' Donovan!" she yelled. She was spitting drunken venom. "Are you going to spend all night swooning all over that *friend* of yours?" I stared at her in disbelief. How on earth had I ever dated anybody as self-centred, illogical and full of double standards? I had tried to resolve things numerous times that evening, to no avail.

Fionnuala had had enough. She sidled over to me, wrapping her body side-on around my hip. Dragging my arm around her waist, she draped one of her own across my hips and the other hand provocatively on my chest between my breasts. I started in surprise and looked down the four-odd inches' height difference to her face beaming up at me with the naughtiest drunken grin I had ever seen her sport. She winked at me. Again. "Swooning all over me, were ye, lover? Well I never!"

"I knew it!" screeched Síofra, in total outrage.

Fionnuala mocked her even further. "What? Ye really thought we shared a one-bedroom flat and never shagged? Get real, ye dumb cow!" Fi sneered. Instinctively I knew that she was on the defensive and sticking up for me. I liked it.

I knew that it was over between Síofra and me. How had I ever gone out with such a vapid brat? The stark contrast between Síofra and Fionnuala prompted a moment of drunken realisation: I needed someone like Fionnuala – interesting, intelligent, fun, caring, someone who's got your back, bloody gorgeous…! Bugger, incoming revival of dangerous crush! This ran deeper than I thought. Confused as hell and suddenly panicky, I ran my fingers frustratedly through my short hair. Fionnuala, as always in tune with my every mood and foible, stroked my lower back gently with her thumb. This time, she was not helping. I was getting seriously hot under the collar.

Misinterpreting my malcontent for worry about her, Síofra smugly placed one hand on her hip and smiled nastily. "What, nothing to say?"

I looked at her, through her, coldly. "Goodbye Síofra." I owed her nothing else.

I walked away, Fionnuala taking my hand, leaving Síofra to stare at the back of our heads as we made for the exit. After collecting our jackets, we headed out into the biting cold of the night. Fionnuala took my hand again and I stiffened slightly, enjoying the sensation way too much. She entwined our fingers, gently, comfortingly, and stroked the back of my hand with her other hand. I glanced at her and sighed, assuming that she was as drunk as I figured I most likely was too.

"I'm sorry," she said quietly. I met her eyes. "I couldn't help it. You know my temper, and seriously, she was treating you..." She took a deep breath to still her anger, and then looked up at me after exhaling deeply. "Are ye sorry it's over?"

That was just it. I felt reborn.

"Not even slightly." I answered thoughtfully. I grinned at her. "You were brilliant back there. When I grow up, I want to be just like you!"

"Eurgh, she's just lucky I didn't knock her out! Anyway, fancy a walk home?"

"Sure you can go the distance in those heels?"

"Always!" She paused. "I meant it when I said that I enjoy playing your damsel in distress." We strolled along in companionable silence, across O'Connell Bridge.

"Fuckin' lezzies!" A sneering male voice accosted us as we passed a late-night fast food shop. Chips in hand, the Neanderthal continued: "Go on, have a nice snog, then we can show you what a real man can do for you." He was joined by two more apes in the doorway.

"Fi," I warned, in a low voice. She ignored me.

"Oi, dickhead!" The sniggering stopped as he turned towards us again. "Fuck off home for a wank, will ye. Get it out of yer system, ye fuckin baboon!"

"What the fuck?!" I heard from the chipper.

Fionnuala looked at me merrily, systematically removed her heels and said, "Run!"

She grabbed my hand again and we sprinted off down the street and on towards Parnell Square. Panting and out of breath, we finally stopped, hands on knees to catch our breath.

"No hot pursuit, then," Fionnuala panted. Little did she know... I stared at her flushed face and sparkling eyes and grinned.

"You are my fucking hero," I laughed. It may have been the drink talking, but Fionnuala straightened, slowly and deliberately, and stepped closer. She cupped my face in her hands. All mirth had disappeared from her expression, replaced by a gravity and anxiety I didn't see often.

"Jay O' Donovan, you numbskull, you've always been mine," she breathed, her body now close enough for me to feel her heat against my abdomen. What on earth was happening?

In my still drunk state of honesty, my hands placed themselves on her hips and I sighed. The contours of her body through the raw silk of her dress made me gasp softly. I was terrified. This was not a random lustful tryst; this was my best friend and *this*, whatever it was, was taking my breath away.

A glimpse of the old sassy Fionnuala glinted through the solemnity of the moment. "So, am I going to have to be the one to kiss you, as well as drag you kicking and screaming out of that closet of yours?"

"Fi—"

"Shut up."

It was the sweetest, most erotic moment of my life. Fionnuala gently pressed her lips to mine. Heat rushed through my body in a wave and I fell against her. There was no doubt that Fionnuala was a very willing participant in this kiss, as illustrated by the guttural moan that escaped her throat into my mouth. Her hand snaked up the back of my neck and into my hair, pulling my face harder against hers. When her lips parted, and her tongue sensuously licked my bottom lip asking permission to enter, I wrapped my arms, vice-like, around her waist and back and opened my mouth to deepen the kiss. I could feel her hips pressed to mine and my knees wobbled precariously. Fionnuala chortled throatily into my mouth and moved her face a couple of inches away from mine. "Steady! A bit drunk, are we?"

"On what I'm not sure," I answered lustily. But when Fionnuala leaned towards me again, I stopped her and stepped away. "What are we doing, Fi?"

She cocked her head to the side and smiled widely at me.

"I don't know about you, Jay, but I'm busy getting seriously turned on by you." She stepped in again, her breath on my neck, lips brushing my earlobe. I summoned my will-power and tried to step away again. Fionnuala held on tighter.

"What?" she mocked good-naturedly. "I've been waiting for my chance with you for, oh, about ten years, Jay. I think I've... we've... waited long enough, don't you?"

"You're... you're gay?" I blinked stupidly at her. How had I not known this?

"I prefer the term 'fluid' actually. And to be honest, only for you, Jay. Only ever for you." The sound of my name on her lips had taken on a whole new meaning and I was way too bloody turned on by her to protest much further.

"Are you sure?" I asked lamely.

Fionnuala shrugged her shoulders cutely. "I don't think I have ever been surer. As I said, dufus," she said with a smile, "I've waited long enough."

Good enough for me. I crashed my body and mouth to hers, forgetting all concerns and reservations in an instant. This beautiful, admirable, compassionate, funny, loyal woman wanted me. To be with me.

I fumbled the key into the lock of our flat door. Fionnuala's arms encircled my waist from behind, her mouth pressed to the base of my neck, dropping heated kisses along the top of my spine. I had not envisioned this scenario earlier this evening; I felt safe. This went infinitely deeper than lust. Clichés aside, this felt like coming home in more ways than the obvious.

Once in our little living room, Fionnuala slowly and deliberately backed me up towards the sofa and pushed me down onto it. In one fluid movement, she hitched up her dress and straddled my thighs. I knew that she liked to be in charge, but I had never envisioned this, even in my wildest dreams.

"Christ, I've wanted you for so bloody long, Jay."

She lowered her mouth to mine again and our mouths met fiercely. I felt Fionnuala's hands in my hair again and she began to gyrate gently on top of me. I tentatively explored the exposed skin of her thighs, running my hands along the softness of her pale Irish skin. My breath caught in my throat as Fionnuala allowed her hand to stray to my chest and I heard her sharp intake of breath as her palm discovered the hardness of my nipples. I opened my eyes and looked up at her, intrigued as to what was running through her mind. She met my eyes when our lips parted briefly, flushed and breathing heavily, her own chest rising and falling deliciously.

"I don't know about you, Fi, but this is not just a roll in the sack for me." She smiled so, so sweetly at me and sat up.

"Ask me then," she said. I looked at her, confused. "Well, you're the one that brought this up! Go on, ask me."

I looked at her curiously and it dawned on me what she wanted. She wanted me to be the one to ask. Simply that.

"Will you be my girlfriend, Fi?" I mumbled self-consciously.

"What? What was that? I can't hear ye!" She giggled, and the vibrations of her body were like electricity against mine.

"You fucker, Fionnuala Kearns! I feel like I'm fifteen again!" I used my hips to lift her off of me and laid her gently on her back on the sofa. "You heard me." I smiled again.

She gazed seriously at me. "Yeh, I did. And yes."

She pulled my body to hers. We fit, so unbelievably well. Her movements against me told me that we were in exactly the same place, body and soul. Ever so gently, I moved my hand lower and Fionnuala's breath hitched. I could feel a heat there that I knew I already adored. This was home. Fionnuala was my home.

###

SARAH BOLGER Originally from Ireland, Sarah is a secondary school English teacher based in Manchester. She is generally to be found with her head firmly ensconced in a book, or dreaming about the next time she will get to do some foreign travel –something she and her wife adore. It was during their most recent trip to Thailand and India on sabbatical that Sarah rediscovered her yearning to write and create; this short story is a product of that period. When not writing, travelling or teaching, she loves being outdoors, sharing a good Rioja and spending time with fabulous family and friends.

ONCE UPON A CARAVAN
Clare Lydon

WHEN DAVID HAD first mooted the idea of a caravan holiday, Stella hadn't been keen. Holidays to her had to be luxurious - soft pillows, crisp sheets and relentless sunshine. She wasn't interested in Formica tables and foam-covered seats. Holidays were a place where you should get away from it all, not add to your daily woes.

Yet here she was. In North Yorkshire, in a caravan park. Clearly, without her knowledge, she'd turned into a walking lesbian cliché. At least she hadn't bought an anorak, even though she knew the odds were she might need one. Rain was forecast every single day.

"Not a caravan park, a luxury holiday park!" David had stated on their way in. "Look, it says so on the sign." He'd leaned over and popped a travel mint into his mouth, before adding: "It's even got a Starbucks." Stella had tried to conjure up her impressed face but found she'd mislaid it on the drive.

David approached the car now. He'd put on a bit of weight in the past couple of months and she could see the outline of his stomach straining over his belt. He still had an impressive head of hair for a man in his late 40s, was still desirable she supposed. She was sure there had to be a caravan-loving woman out there who could make her brother happy.

David smiled and waved as he got nearer, brandishing what she assumed was the caravan key in his right hand. There was no escape now. He opened the door to his red Fiesta and sat down in the driver's seat, rubbing his hands together as he spoke.

"Right, we're number 54. Over towards the far right. And guess what?" His face shone with excitement: this, after all, was David's Disneyland.

"What?" she asked.

"I upgraded us!" He sat back to bask in his upgraded glory. "Isn't that great?"

Stella considered his question. "Does it mean we get greeted at the door with Champagne?"

David gave her a stare that told her he'd overlook her sarcasm this one time. "You'll see," he said, rubbing her right knee before starting the car. "You'll be amazed - it's even got a veranda. A veranda!"

Stella looked straight ahead as they set off down the road. To their left, the cliffs stopped abruptly, leading down to miles of oak-coloured sand, the sea sparkling like a field of diamonds under the early afternoon sun. They passed a wooden stall selling buckets, spades and ice cream to holiday-makers, along with a variety of sunhats and the ever-present sturdy windbreakers. To their right, caravans stood reverently still, a portrait of pastel colours with sinister metal edges. She hoped theirs was blue, her favourite colour. Or failing that, custard yellow.

It was certainly a step up from the caravan holidays of her youth, but it still wasn't Valencia, Stella's destination of choice. She and Alex had spoken of going last year, but had never managed it. They were unlikely to ever go now, given the circumstances. So she'd said yes to David and the flip of a coin had decided their holiday fate: bracing North Yorkshire it was. Stella closed her eyes and conjured visions of tapas, sun-kissed streets and ice cold beers on sunny piazzas. But at least there was a Starbucks.

David swung the car neatly into a space next to a grey Range Rover and tugged on the handbrake. "I think it's that one," he said, pointing. His door was open and he was trying not to run towards the cream caravan jutting out from the rest, noticeable for its lack of colour. He turned as he approached and gave Stella a thumbs-up.

"Cream," she muttered. "Figures."

Stella unclicked her seatbelt, the metal buckle grazing her nose. She swore lightly as she got out of the car, smoothing down her blue-and-white striped top, tucking her unruly curls behind her ears as the wind whipped them sharply. David had disappeared, but she knew it would only be a matter of seconds before he was back again. She walked past the caravan next to theirs. Inside, a young boy had an intense look of concentration on his face as he played cards with an older man. She remembered doing the same with her granddad as a young girl.

And then there was David, hanging out of the caravan door, features animated beyond his control.

"Oh my god, you have to see this!" he said, shaking his head. "Everything is so small!" He was yelping now. David disappeared again and she followed him in. She had to agree: everything was so small, and she imagined again how much larger everything was in Valencia. Sunnier. Hotter. Improved.

"I'm going to make a cuppa - you want one?" he asked.

But Stella was barely aware of him now. The rushing had taken over her head and she didn't know how to stop it. She saw Alex in every surface, saw her outline in the veins on the back of her hand. Her body ached for her as she sat on the caravan-sized sofa. She had to put her hand out to stop herself from falling, even though she was sitting down.

"Stella? Stella?" David's voice was fizzing around her, but she wasn't sure where it started or where it ended. "Sweetheart, it's ok. You're fine. *I'm here.*" David gently rubbed her palms with his thumbs. His green eyes were wide in front of her, his face a question mark of concern.

"I..." she began, before shaking her head. "It's just a bit stuffy in here. I think I need some air."

Stella stood up with his help and walked slowly to the open door, feeling the cooling sea breeze as she put one foot onto the corrugated iron step. However, David was soon distracted by the tiny bedroom and the shoe-horned bathroom to the right of the front door.

"So tiny but big enough!" he said. "Amazing isn't it?"

Stella thought she might be sick. "Can I catch my breath first?" she said.

David's face fell. "I'll put the kettle on," he said, turning back inside, before stopping. He clicked his fingers together and pursed his lips. "We don't have any milk."

Stella held up her hand. "I'll go," she said. "There must be a shop here." She ducked back inside before he could argue and grabbed her red handbag, which seemed altogether out of place in this environment.

It was good to be out in the fresh air, good to be out of the car, out of the caravan, with room to breathe. She passed some recycling bins on her way to the cliff top, taking in the coastal views that spread out on both sides of her for miles. She should have put her cardigan on, as the wind was needling her neck, goosebumps appearing on her arms despite the bright sun in the sky above. This was still May and she was still in Yorkshire.

She drank in the majesty of the views and pondered how ironic it was to be in Yorkshire but *without* Alex. Alex had loved to walk, probably still did. Assuming she was still alive. Alex loved the ruggedness of the north, loved holidaying without guaranteed sunshine.

Over the years, Stella had maintained it was healthy to have separate interests and not to live in each other's pockets, so Alex had walked alone or with friends. Until the day her walking had completely overtaken her and she'd started and never looked back, leaving Stella and their entire life behind after seven years together. Six months and still not a word.

Stella shivered as she turned from the cliff top, crossing her arms in front of her body to shield her from the elements. She almost walked straight into two older lesbians, clad in purple and green outdoor wear, sturdy boots, walking sticks and rucksacks. They smiled and gave her a knowing look, which she returned. *Did they know where Alex was?*

Stella walked briskly now, back across the road and through the maze of caravans. Within five minutes she was spat out into the central concourse that held the park office, as well as the promised Starbucks, a mini-market and a pub & grill, all housed in low-rise square boxes.

A brightly coloured playground sat in the middle of this urban planner's nightmare, with children weaving in and out of adults, chairs and tables. The camp office had neon flags outside it that were fluttering madly in the breeze, offering caravans for sale, from Deluxe to Platinum. What type had David upgraded to? It didn't seem to fit any of the categories on offer.

Stella walked around the mass of families and into the cooling air conditioning of the mini-market. A bakery section lured her in with its freshly baked smell and she grabbed two Danish pastries as a holiday treat. Then she set off round the shop clutching a dented wire basket, the beginnings of a headache forming on the outskirts of her brain. She kept having to remind herself she was on holiday and this was fun.

Stella was pondering an on-offer Pinot Grigio she thought might take the edge off the coming evening when she noticed her. Stella loved feet and hers were foot model-good: pearl nails painted and styled to perfection atop smooth, tanned skin. Stella gulped as she stood next to the woman, still peering down at the wine selection, taking in her scent as she did. She recognised it but couldn't place it, yet the perfume filled Stella's nostrils beautifully.

The woman turned suddenly, completely unaware of Stella's presence, and lifted a wine bottle straight into Stella's bent head, smack into her cheekbone. There was a crack, and Stella's head snapped backwards, along with her body. She staggered sideways into a stocky man, bouncing off him with ease. Being terribly British, Stella mumbled an apology, clutching the side of her face with one hand, still gripping her basket with the other. Was this all part of the shopping experience in caravan parks? She was sure it didn't happen in Valencia.

"Oh my god, I'm so sorry!" The woman had alarm pasted across her features as she squinted at Stella. "Are you hurt? It sounded like it hurt. It was my fault, not looking where I was going…"

Stella was nodding her head, even though it was throbbing and it hurt to do so. She straightened up and gingerly lifted her hand from her eye. It felt like it had swollen to the size of one of the smaller caravans.

"God, you're bleeding," the woman said. Her voice was low, bass like. She replaced her wine in the chiller cabinet and took a packet of tissues from a bag slung over her shoulder, offering a handful to

Stella who gratefully accepted them. Then the woman reached down and removed the basket Stella was still holding.

"Wait here, I'll be back," the woman said.

Stella peered out of her good eye and saw the woman at the cash desk, ensuring their baskets were stashed. She was wearing denim shorts and a red top, and her arms were as tanned as her feet. The woman had that bronzed look about her that comes from fresh air, hard work and contentment. Stella wondered if she was lifeguard, or perhaps a gardener. Stella had always quite fancied dating a gardener. She blamed Charlie Dimmock.

The woman approached her now looking concerned, sweeping her short brown hair off her face even though it was nowhere near her face and hadn't moved. Nervous habit, Stella noted.

"Right," the woman said. "How about you come back to my caravan – it's just round the corner – I'll make you a cup of tea and clean you up. You can come and pick up your shopping after that. And hopefully by then, you'll only be able to see one of me. Sound like a plan?"

Stella was shivering from shock and the thought of tea was warming. She nodded and allowed the woman to steer her out of the shop, around the playground and over towards a baby blue caravan that looked twice the size of theirs, and was. Inside, there was a breakfast bar, a giant (distinctly un-caravan-like) sofa and a plush kitchen that sparkled with wealth. Did this woman own the caravan park?

"Sit, please," she said, gently easing Stella on to the sofa with a hand on the small of her back and one on her elbow. The physical contact was pleasurable to Stella's abandoned body and she jolted from it, her eyes meeting the woman's as she sat. The moment hung in the air and the woman knelt before her, easing the tissues out of her hand.

Stella winced at the stain of red on white.

The woman cupped her chin softly and Stella swallowed hard, feeling a pang of desire zap down her body. She willed herself to hold it together and not become a cliché, falling apart in front of the first attractive woman to touch her since Alex.

"It's not too bad; hopefully it's just a bruise. And you've stopped bleeding too. Does your cheekbone feel ok?" the woman asked.

Stella took in the fine hairs on the woman's cheek, the pink rouge of her lips. She put her hand up to her cheek and felt along the bone. "A bit sore, but not broken I don't think." She exhaled. "I'm Stella by the way."

"Casey," the woman smiled. "Let me make you that cup of tea. Restorative power, tea." Casey pushed herself up off her tanned thighs to her full height and walked to the kitchen. She filled the kettle, its noise polluting the limited caravan air.

"So is this your party trick to pick up women?" Stella asked. She swivelled her head towards the kitchen.

Casey gave her a smile of recognition. "I'm usually a bit more old-fashioned about these things," she said. "You know, drinks, dinner and some chat before I get them back here." Casey winked. "But this clearly works just as well..."

Stella let out a bark of laughter, but the movement hurt her face and she winced.

Casey winced right back at her. "You might not want to do that for a while. No watching funny films for a bit either - just depressing films for you, ok? Doctor's orders."

Stella put her hand to her brow and gave Casey a salute. "Yes sir." Stella paused. "So are you a doctor? Or just a friendly assailant?"

Casey smiled and it lit up her face, reaching from her mouth to her eyes and beyond. "Not a medical doctor, no. I'm a doctor of philosophy, specialising in medical research. But my doctorly advice still stands."

There was silence then apart from the sound of teabags being squeezed and milk being glugged.

"Sugar?" Casey asked, again sweeping back some imaginary hair.

Stella shook her head. "Sweet enough." *When did she become such a brazen flirt?*

"So it seems."

Casey rounded the breakfast bar, put the mugs of tea on the floor and sank into the sofa beside Stella, sighing. "I really am sorry you know – about the whole smashing you in the face with a wine bottle thing." She paused, before turning her body to face Stella. "But how about I make it up to you later – do you fancy a drink in the bar?" Casey held Stella's gaze and it was all it took.

Stella nodded gently, spellbound. "I'd love to. But I should warn you – I'm here with my brother so you might have to meet him too." Stella paused. "And he *loves* caravans, so be prepared."

"And you don't I take it?" Casey's eyes raked Stella's body.

Stella's skin prickled with desire. "I wasn't really feeling it this morning, but now, having been bottled, I feel like I'm really entering into the spirit of it," Stella said.

"I'm pleased," Casey replied, a smile playing on her lips. "Some bad entertainment and sub-standard food this evening and you'll truly have embraced the whole experience."

Stella smiled carefully. "Although if we had a caravan like this, maybe I wouldn't be so hesitant. Since when did caravans have fireplaces for god's sakes?"

Casey chuckled. "What can I say? Some people's families have holiday homes in the South of France or Portugal, mine chose a caravan in Filey. But it's free and far from the madding crowds." She shrugged. "I like it."

Stella's breath quickened as her gaze travelled Casey's body, taking in the outline of her full breasts, her flat stomach. She licked her lips, then took a sip of her tea for something to do.

They sat staring at each other, electricity crackling between them.

Stella had a powerful urge to bruise Casey's lips, slide her tongue into her inviting mouth. She gulped before she acted on instinct.

"Can I use your bathroom, just to check the damage?" Stella asked, breaking the tension.

Casey nodded and sprang up from the sofa. "Past the front door, on the right."

Stella moved swiftly, glimpsing the sizeable double bedroom with pure white sheets and an en-suite straight ahead, her mind jumping ahead and her body reacting before she could tell it to slow down. She rushed into the bathroom, locked the door and looked in the mirror, surveying the damage.

Her right cheek had a red and purple hue and she thought she might get a black eye tomorrow, which she was secretly hoping for. She'd never had a black eye before and had always thought they looked sexy. Stella ran the cold water and splashed it on her face. She carefully patted dry before eyeballing herself in the mirror.

"What are you doing?" she asked herself. "You don't even know this woman." But her face followed her heart and broke into a shy smile. Who would have thought she'd meet somebody in a caravan park? David would be thrilled.

David. She really ought to get back as he was probably wondering where on earth she'd got to. That is, if he'd got over how incredible the caravan was yet. Stella blinked twice, shook her head at her reflection and unlocked the bathroom door.

Casey was standing at the breakfast bar when she emerged, holding out her mug of tea.

"Everything all right?"

Stella nodded. "I think I'll live." She took a large gulp of her tea, then put her mug on the counter. "I really should go – I only nipped out to get some milk for our tea. My brother will think I've been kidnapped."

Casey smiled. "Guilty as charged." She walked over and pushed the front door open for Stella. "Seven o'clock in the bar?"

Stella looked at her watch – only three hours till her first ever date with her brother in tow. "I'll look forward to it," she said.

Stella reached out and grazed Casey's arm lightly with her hand – the compulsion to touch her was overwhelming. Casey's heated gaze followed Stella as she stepped out of the caravan, her heart thumping in her chest.

Perhaps caravanning wasn't so bad after all.

CLARE LYDON's debut novel, *London Calling*, was an Amazon No.1 best-seller in the UK, Canada and Australia. Her second novel, *The Long Weekend*, was released this autumn. Clare's a Virgo, a guitar anti-hero, karaoke queen and Curly Wurly devotee. She's also never been on holiday in a caravan park and her wife hopes it stays that way.

Connect with Clare at www.clarelydon.co.uk or on Twitter @clarelydon

SONG OF THE SEA
Crin Claxton

I STOPPED AT the harbour and looked out to sea. My lungs opened, drinking in the salt air. Left and right was an expanse of grey green water rolling and turning under the same colour sky. Sunlight, with only a touch of warmth in it, played off the foaming waves.

Bird cry distracted me: the tsee-tsee-tsee of a blue tit calling from the skeleton arms of a peach tree. The bird's vibrant yellow chest was puffed up against the cold. It seemed intent on catching my eye. Then with a leap, it swooped off across the sky. I was headed in the same direction, so I followed, amused that the bird didn't outstretch me.

I was house-sitting a place in Nelson Road, in Whitstable. I was lucky to stumble across it, because my friend Gill's directions said to head into town, away from the beach. Fortunately I'd got distracted following the little blue tit as it flew ahead, drawing me closer and closer to the sea. I'd almost passed the house by, when I saw *Song of the Sea* in fading, hand-painted lettering on a neatly cut square of wood.

An ancient trailing rose wound around the door frame. To my amazement the bush was abundant with large, dark red roses, their petals full and yielding. I pulled a dusky head under my nose. The perfume was startlingly sweet in the crisp March air.

The front door opened straight into a sitting room. Two old brown leather armchairs sat in front of a fireplace, with wood laid out for a fire. There were bookshelves dotted with books and a small wooden table squeezed in the corner, and that was it. There was no music system or TV, and nothing that looked remotely like a router. I frowned. Gill could have warned me. The sitting room led onto to a small kitchen. The fridge looked old, like something out of the sixties. I had a quick look. There was nothing inside but loads of ice, spilling over from a tiny freezer compartment.

The stairs were next to the kitchen and the other side of them a bathroom. There was no shower, just a big old-fashioned bath with feet. There was one small window, high up over the bath that was cranked open a touch. I liked the blue and green tiles on the wall by the bath and around a square Victorian sink. They had a mother of pearl finish that glistened even in the dim light. The sound of waves turning outside drifted through the window.

Up a set of narrow, winding stairs were two bedrooms. The front one contained a double bed, an old wooden wardrobe and a dressing table with an old silver brush and comb set on it. The cottage didn't seem like my friend Gill's kind of place. It was like an old lady lived there, one who hadn't updated the house in a long time. The other bedroom was smaller with a single bed and a desk. The sea was loud in the small bedroom. I could see it out the window. And there was the little bird again, sitting on top of the outhouse roof in the yard below.

Outside, I opened the door to the outbuilding to find a toilet. I realised it was the only toilet. I frowned, imagining having to creep out in the middle of the night to use it. The waves sounded like they were practically lapping the fence.

I stepped through the back gate and straight onto shingle.

The beach was pinky-brown with dark wood breakers at each edge. As I walked towards the water the pebbles sloped down, getting smaller and smaller, until they became warm gritty sand. Then the beach flattened out, turning into a marsh of dark green seaweed, grey mud and shallow water the colour of slate. It was low tide.

I sat down, lulled by the rolling waves. They streamed up the beach and then drew back into the ocean. The tide was coming in. I got up when I heard someone singing a haunting melody.

I walked towards the sound. It blew against my face, blending with the wind. The song had the rise and fall of waves in it somehow and a high haunting quality like gulls calling.

The singer stood at the water's edge on a deserted stretch of beach. She looked out to sea at the darkening sky. The sun was reduced to fiery fingers reaching for the horizon.

I stopped a few metres away.

The singer glanced my way and smiled. Then she turned back to the sea, still singing.

The wind blew her long hair straight back behind her like a sail. Her voice drifted across the water and seemed to return on the waves as they crashed home. She had a short-sleeved blue dress on and a pearl necklace. She was bare foot. Her pale skin had no goose-bumps.

When the song ended she turned.

"Hello. I'm Nina," I said. "Your voice is beautiful."

"I'm Mari. And thank you. Did you like the song?"

I nodded, suddenly tongue-tied.

"Why don't you sing with me?"

"Oh I don't know about that. I don't sing."

"But we're the only people here. You can even come and stand next to me if you like." She smiled, like she was teasing me gently. "That way our voices will blend better."

"But I don't know the song." I said, moving next to her.

"Improvise," she said and started singing.

I was self-conscious at first, sure I would ruin the song. But gradually the music got to me. First I was humming and then I was full-on, open-mouthed singing. Gulls flew overhead, calling. Mari's voice shifted and it was like she was singing with the gulls. We all sang together. It felt like a celebration of the day: of air to fly in, water to swim and fish in, land to walk on. It was exhilarating.

I sang till I was hoarse. When we stopped it sounded quiet. I grinned at Mari.

"That was amazing!"

She nodded and smiled back at me. "It's a shame but I have to go now, Nina."

I shrugged. "Ok. Thanks for the singing, I enjoyed it."

"So did I. Hope to see you again." Mari walked away through the waves at the shore's edge.

It took me half an hour to get back, stopping for fish and chips on the way. It was six o'clock and almost dark. I'd left the cottage about two. Where had four hours gone? There was a puddle of water on the floor by the fridge. It smelled like sea water.

I ate at the little table in the sitting room. The silence wrapped itself gently around me. I couldn't remember the last time I'd eaten without talking to someone, or without the TV on.

I built a fire, turned all the lights out and watched the flames. I wondered if the cottage was damp because there looked to be steam around the edges of the flickering light. My eyelids began to droop. I thought I should go to bed...in a minute.

When I opened my eyes the fire had burnt right down to embers.

I went outside to the toilet. Frost glistened on the outhouse roof. The wind tugged at the back gate.

As I came out of the outhouse the gate swung open and Mari was standing there. Her skin was blue in the frosty moonlight. Somehow I wasn't surprised to see her.

"Come in," I said.

She went inside and straight upstairs to the back bedroom where the noise of the sea was loudest. I took my clothes off and left them where they fell. Mari undressed too, with a sensual confidence. Her body shone like she was oiled.

She went to the bed and I got in next to her. She was cold. God knows how long she'd been standing out on the beach. I pulled her to me, to warm her, and felt her shiver.

"You feel good," she whispered.

As I kissed her, her cold hands swept over my body, leaving icy trails. They were good icy trails. I caressed her, marvelling at how soft she was. She smelt of salt. We moved together all night, all night till the moon set and daylight crept under the window. I wrapped myself around her and slept.

I woke up past mid-morning alone and wondered if I'd dreamt the whole thing. Why would Mari be walking about on the beach in the middle of the night? My body didn't feel like I'd dreamt it. I'd either had sex with someone, or I'd had a very weird hallucinogenic experience I hadn't had to pay for.

I decided to get out and explore the area. I picked up my book and drawing pad, grabbed some food and stepped out the back way turning west, away from the town.

I walked along the shingle, heading nowhere in particular. Stones crunched under my trainers. The wind blew, waves rose and fell, gulls called and tied-up boats rattled eerily.

I found a spot looking across the water to the little Isle of Sheppey, where it was light, breezy and sunny. I got out my book and settled into the story.

I was gazing across at the island in the late afternoon sun when an old lady came walking along the beach. She stopped beside me.

"This is a pretty spot," she remarked.

"It's nice and quiet." I nodded.

"It's where they used to collect the salt, you know," she told me.

"Oh?"

"Yes." She looked like the kind of woman who walked the beach every day. "They used to collect it in pans, over there, letting the water evaporate to leave the salt."

"Really." I followed her gaze, trying to imagine Whitstable in those days. The job she described must have been hard and was probably paid a pittance.

"You want to be careful of sea spirits."

"Sea spirits?" I searched the old lady's face. Her brown, bird-like eyes fixed on mine.

"Yes sea spirits. Watch out for them. Especially near the water's edge."

She turned and started walking away. I watched her go, wondering what sea spirits were. Some kind of jelly fish probably.

As the woman disappeared from my view, dark clouds came rolling over the horizon. I ran to the cottage, getting back as the sky darkened and spots of rain began to fall.

Lights were already on inside. Mari was in the kitchen, putting the finishing touches to a salad.

"Hi, Nina." She kissed me and took my jacket.

"Mari! Last night did happen then?"

She looked at me, the way someone looks at you when they think you're a little strange. "Of course it did. Why do you ask?"

I was so relieved I smiled and said: "It doesn't matter."

"Follow me." She took me to the bathroom where she had already run a bath. Blue-green candles flickered everywhere. The bath smelt of fruit, flowers and sea salt.

I got into the warm, sweet-smelling water and Mari brought food from the kitchen. She got in the bath with me. Her curvy body was beautiful: silk soft and powerful.

She fed me prawns and crab, kelp bread and salad. She fed me piece by piece, sometimes from her own mouth so we were all mixed up with each other. She poured wine into my mouth from her glass and from her mouth till I didn't know where she ended and I began. And when the wine was gone, she played with my body, rocking the bath water and causing a mini tidal wave to consume me.

When the bath was cold Mari wanted to go into the back bedroom again so that she could hear the sea. I thought that was romantic. I didn't mind being closer to her in the smaller bed. I was drunk on love. Mari encouraged it. We laughed and talked. I stroked her body wide-eyed in the middle of the night, awake and counting my blessings.

I wasn't surprised she wasn't there when I woke up. I didn't mind. I knew she'd be back.

I lay in bed for a long time. The scent of her was on the sheets. I dug out my book, but Mari was all I could think about.

Mari came each night around sunset, always bringing food, often bringing flowers. I presumed she went to work each day but I didn't ask. I didn't ask where she lived. I never thought about those things when we were together. I switched on when Mari came home. I went from dreamy to full-throttle and all it took was the squeak of the gate and her voice calling my name.

One night, Mari asked: "What did you do today, Nina?"

We were sitting at the table in the sitting room. I'd decorated it earlier with candles, flowers and shells that Mari had brought to the house. It was the first time she'd asked me anything like that. I tried to remember what I'd done. I couldn't think of anything.

"Nothing much," I said after a while.

"Did you go out?"

I shook my head.

"Why not?"

Her question annoyed me. It felt like an interrogation. I turned from the table to tell her to mind her own business. I stopped short at the most dazzling smile.

"I don't know Mari, just tired I guess. I'll go out tomorrow."

"That's a good idea," she said.

But I didn't go out the next day. When she left me I sulked. I was getting bored on my own and I didn't understand why Mari wouldn't stay with me. I couldn't read, couldn't draw. I couldn't understand why I always woke up after Mari had gone. I wondered what was wrong with me and whether I was making a fool of myself. If I was, it was too late. I was completely hers. I would wait for her forever, if she made me.

A small kernel of resistance glowed within me. And from that kernel I sulked.

When Mari got home I was moody and childish. She refused to be drawn into an argument, though I pushed her. I refused to be pulled upstairs to the bathroom or distracted by trinkets from the sea and shellfish.

"If you loved me, you'd want to be with me," I said, the tension in my hands forcing them rigid.

Mari looked sad. "Nina, you know, love and water are very alike." She held me, stroking my hair.

My body responded immediately, wanting her even through my hurt feelings.

"If you hold water gently in a cupped hand you can hold it for a while. But if you try to grasp it in your fist it slips through your fingers."

I kissed her, stopping the words from her lips. *Oh Mari, how I loved you that night. There was nothing I wouldn't have done for you.* I held her hand to my lips, closed my eyes and blessed the day she was born on. I let her lead me upstairs, pushed misgivings away and gave her everything I had to give.

The next morning I woke up sure she would stay. She was getting dressed. My heart sank. *How can she work every day; isn't this Sunday?* I couldn't be sure, there was no TV or radio. I hadn't bought a paper for days. I'd let my mobile run down and hadn't bothered to charge it.

I let her go, without comment. I went to the window and watched her walk along the beach until she was far into the distance.

I watched the beach for a moment when she was out of sight. It was overcast. The ocean was grey and fretful. Boat chains rattled hard in a strong sea breeze. I tasted the salt spray flung by the wind at the house.

I shut the window and turned to the room. I narrowed my eyes at the tiny space.

It's ridiculous us sleeping in a single bed every night. I'm going in that double bed tonight, even if she doesn't!

My rebellious thought felt good. It felt delicious, in fact. It was the first independent thought I'd had in days.

I got dressed quickly.

Where does she go every day, anyway? I'm not going to stay shut up in this house, like a lovesick puppy.

Outside, the beach seemed bigger than before. The wind was strong and I let it carry me. I felt powerful. I walked as fast as I could. Suddenly I had energy. I felt it released from some place I'd been holding it.

I ran, the wind behind me, my feet so light on the shingle I hardly felt it. I leapt over wooden breakers without getting a splinter in my hand.

At the harbour suddenly people were all around me. It felt like hundreds, it was probably twenty. Really I wanted to be there with

Mari. But she'd never wanted to leave the house together. *She must be ashamed of me.*

With a strange and unreasonable anger I walked back to the cottage. The wind was against me and I took it personally. It really was bloody freezing in Whitstable. There was always the wind howling and the beached boats clanking. The damned wind forever blowing across endless space, with nothing to hold it back, till it worked itself into a fury.

I was raging so much I walked right past the cottage. I realised when I got to the marshy beach I'd sat and read on. I wasn't happy about having to walk back. The wind was behind me once more but it pushed me too fast. I was in a foul mood.

I got to where the house should be but it wasn't there.

I looked left and right. Everything about the beach was the same: the breakers, the upside down boat with flaking red paint moored to a rusting buoy.

There was a building exactly where Song of the Sea should be. There was no backyard, no outside toilet. A middle-aged woman peered out the window. She looked anxious. I realised I was staring. I went round to the front of the house to check. It had a number, but no name on it. It was bigger than Gill's cottage, with freshly painted weather-boarding. A man in white overalls was at work painting a downstairs window frame.

My heart raced as I walked back along the beach. I was sure I'd got lost. I walked as far as the harbour but the house was nowhere to be seen. I remembered from Gill's directions that her place was on Nelson Road.

I left the Visitors' Centre with a map. Nelson Road turned away from the beach but I went down it anyway.

Halfway down the road, I found Song of the Sea. But it wasn't my Song of the Sea. It was a brick built, bay-windowed Edwardian terraced house.

I walked up the path. My hand shook as I pulled Gill's keys from my pocket.

They fitted the lock.

I opened the door and stepped into the hall.

The first door to the right led into a sitting room. I turned on the TV and flicked to a news channel to get the date.

The date was twelve days after I'd arrived.

Where have I been staying?

In the kitchen I checked the fridge and the bin. Both were empty.

Upstairs in one of the bedrooms I found my bag, on the floor, unopened. In shock I got into bed. I lay shivering until I fell asleep.

In the morning I had the flu. I woke with an ache inside me so bad it made me physically sick. I retched on an empty stomach on my knees in the bathroom.

I couldn't stay. Weak and shaking, I picked up my bag and headed for the train station.

On the high street I stopped outside a funky little cafe and decided to go in. As I opened the door the scent of coffee and toasted panini hit my nostrils. The Arctic Monkeys were playing in the background, just under hum drum chatter that felt familiar and normal. It was just what I needed. Relief flooded through me.

I sipped a strong, black coffee and hardly knew what to think. Wherever I'd been, whoever Mari was, the time with her was like a long, weird dream. And it was gone.

At the till, I searched for loose change. I tapped the top pocket of my shirt. There was something hard in there. I opened my fist in the sunlight pouring through the big plate glass window.

Two silver grey pearls glistened in the palm of my hand.

CRIN CLAXTON is the author of the vampire novel *Scarlet Thirst* and the Foreword Indie Fab winning (2013) ghost mystery *The Supernatural Detective*. Short stories have been published by Diva Books, Bella Books, Bold Strokes Books, Diva magazine and Carve webzine. S/he has recipes in *The Butch Cook Book*. Poems have been published by Onlywomen Press and La Pluma. *Death's Doorway*, the next Supernatural Detective series novel, is due out June 2015.

Crin is a lighting designer for theatre. S/he was Festival Director for the York Lesbian Arts Festival 2007-2009. S/he lives in London.

Author of The Supernatural Detective, a girl meets girl meets ghosts mystery

IndieFab Award Winner 2013!

Scarlet Thirst sexy vampire thriller

www.crinclaxton.com/

Look out for the next Supernatural Detective mystery *Death's Doorway* out June 2015

THE DOLLY PARTON FAN CLUB DENY ANY CONNECTION
Angela Clerkin

CHEN, THE SMALL, middle-aged security guard, standing just inside the door of the building society is scratching his neck. Saturday, 3.18pm. This is an everyday scene: customers depositing and withdrawing their hard-earned cash, bank tellers watching the clock and the manager flirting with one of the young midriff-on-show mothers. Suddenly four figures dressed as Dolly Parton burst through the doors.

Chen is on red alert and rushes towards the Dollys. There is a flurry of blonde wigs, confused customers, surprised bank tellers, a stunned manager and two bags full of cash.

Minutes later, four Dolly Partons are running down the alleyway beside the building society towards their black BMW getaway car. And later that evening Babs, the hairdresser, almost chokes on her oxtail soup as she watches the Six O'Clock News: "...Two hundred and fifty thousand pounds stolen from the Santander Building Society in Basildon. A note was left by the robbers saying: 'The Dolly Parton Fan Club Deny Any Connection'."

10 DAYS EARLIER

Bubbly, bottle-blonde Rinky was swinging her hips along to Dolly Parton's *Love is like a Butterfly* playing on the radio. With one hand she expertly jooshed her customer's new perm with an infrared hairdryer, and with the other she held a mobile phone to her ear, pacifying an irate customer.

"I'm ever so sorry, Mrs...I did try and warn...I don't think that's strictly true...Green? Oh dear...I agree, not ideal for a seventy-year-old..." Rinky bit her lip as a tirade of squeaky shouting travelled down the line.

"Put it down, Rinky, you're too soft," whispered Babs from the sidelines.

"I can't," replied her employee. Babs shook her head as Rinky turned up her Pollyanna-style persona to turbo charge.

"Pop in tomorrow and I'll try to wash it out...Ok, free of charge. And I promise to give you the best blow job of your life!" An oblivious Rinky ended the call, all smiles.

Rinky had been Babs' assistant for over five years and she loved working at Curl Up and Dye. Her sunny, glass-half-full disposition complemented and contrasted with Babs' tell-it-like-it-is temperament. "Sometimes it's important to get angry, Rinky. Being angry at an injustice, at unacceptable behaviour, is not only not bad, it's essential." She was saved from a lengthy 'life lecture' when the courier stepped through the door carrying a ribboned box. Rinky guessed immediately it was a present from her boyfriend Alex and squealed as she pulled out a little black dress.

"What's he after?" said Babs through pursed lips.

"I think he's going to propose!" Babs raised her eyebrow and Rinky was quick to explain. "It's obvious! Black dress, white dress!!" What was obvious to Babs was that the slimy Alex was working some sort of an angle. She searched the discarded box for an accompanying card and quickly discovered his motive.

§

The red pin icon on Google Maps marked the Santander on East Walk in Basildon town centre. Grace used her finger and thumb to enlarge the map on her iPhone as she perched precariously on Jimmy's hospital bed. She was reluctantly flirting with the idea of the robbery but her best friend was deadly serious. As was his condition. Jimmy was hospitalised after yet another crisis caused by his Sickle Cell Anaemia and he was desperate to go to the specialist centre in Oakland, California, which he couldn't afford. He was pinning his survival hopes on his best mate Grace, her ex-girlfriend Theresa and younger sister Martina pulling off the robbery - he knew the odds weren't good.

To start with, fifteen-year-old Martina had already blabbed to a girl at school she wanted to impress, and added to that, Theresa was the only one with relevant experience. She had spent three years in a Young Offenders Institute for multiple theft. And finally Grace was nursing a broken heart: the split with Theresa was only ten days old. But Jimmy was determined and had drawn up detailed plans for "a harmless, victimless crime. No violence, just a quick in and out, Bob's your uncle, Fanny's your aunt and you're taking me to Oakland!"

§

A big red hat and a laundry bag full of hairdryers were the accessories Rinky had paired with her LBD, but trying to keep the hat on while extracting the bag from the back seat of the black BMW was proving challenging. An irritated Alex in his new Paul Smith suit stood by watching, not helping. "Come on, we're late," he called over his shoulder as he marched ahead. The hairdresser tottered behind him, still hopeful for a proposal.

Preparations for the launch party were in full swing as Rinky and her boyfriend entered the brightly lit club. Various people needing decisions made a beeline for Alex, including his young new PA. Alex patted Rinky's bottom and packed her off backstage to get the waitresses primped.

The dressing room smelt of hairspray and perfumed bodies tightly packed in a tiny space. The thirteen waitresses, all wearing silver crop tops and miniskirts were happily having their hair backcombed to the max. Except for an unhappy Grace, whose small afro did not want to transform into an 'Amy Winehouse beehive'. As Rinky entered, she immediately instructed the fifteen-year-old apprentice to fetch the cocktail trays while she finished off and deftly set about damage limitation.

"Bit of a pig's ear, I'm afraid."

"Thank you!" grinned Grace.

Rinky laughed. "I meant the hair, not you! I think you're beautiful."

Rinky expertly teased and combed. Bending down to catch some of Grace's hair at the back, she sniffed her neck.

"Hmmm. Obsession for Men. Snap!" She put her wrist under Grace's nose to sniff. "I bought it for my boyfriend for Christmas."

"Shame!" Grace winked at the hairdresser.

"Are you flirting with me?!" Rinky's eyes were sparkling, daring.

"Are you flirting with me?!" countered Grace. They both laughed. Rinky asked her if she was a fan of Dolly Parton. For her, this was a question that determined a person's worth, and unfortunately Grace failed. But despite this serious hitch the two women continued chatting and laughing until the expert hairdresser had completed her creation, "a gorgeous silk purse!" Rinky grabbed a couple of cosmopolitans from the tray by her side and announced a toast. "To an auspicious evening." They clinked their glasses and downed their drinks. Three hours later both Rinky and Grace's lives had coincidentally become auspicious, but not in the way either of them wanted.

A tray of cocktails was held in the air above the lively crowd by the small woman with the beautifully styled afro. The party was full of gyrating revellers and the drinks were quickly disappearing into greedy hands and down ravenous throats. A well-oiled Alex took the last two mojitos and planted a slobbery kiss on his pretty young PA's mouth. Grace was immediately reloaded with another tray and she continued weaving through the throng. Her mobile phone was buzzing in her pocket but she didn't have a free hand to check it; she hoped it wasn't anything important.

The beat of the music was calling Rinky and she enthusiastically joined the party having packed the last of the hairdryers away. In the distance she caught a glimpse of Alex chatting to his PA. She waved and tried to get his attention before she was swung around by an enormous man who decided she would be his dancing partner. Another man, another dancing partner, another brief glimpse of Alex, this time over by the door. When she finally made her way to the exit, the bouncer informed her that Alex had just left. A confused Rinky ran outside and saw his car pulling away. Alex was in the driving seat, but he wasn't alone. Rinky was rooted to the spot, uncomprehending. Why would Alex leave his own launch party with his PA? A panicked Grace came out of the club and ran past Rinky. She was clutching her mobile phone and coat, arm raised, flagging down a taxi. "Basildon Hospital, please."

§

The early morning sun peeped through the hospital blinds where the heart monitor beeped a little too fast. Oxygen was fed through a nose tube, and an intravenous drip carrying strong pain killers was attached Jimmy's left arm. An exhausted Grace held Jimmy's right hand. It had been a long and scary night.

§

Over the next few days, Grace was in overdrive organising the robbery. She was resolved to help Jimmy, and no amount of waitressing work was ever going to be enough to get him to Oakland. Theresa was hyped, fuelled by her own mounting debts and the hope that the excitement might reignite the passion between them. She supplied the replica guns which everyone agreed looked ridiculous close up and the plan was nearly abandoned. But desperate times called for desperate measures and soon they were poring over maps and planned escape routes. Alison had come up trumps, not only with the get-away car (her mum's Vauxhall Astra), but also with borrowed keys to her aunt's empty cottage in the Lake District, a hide-out while the heat was on in Basildon.

§

Three days after the launch party and Rinky was still curled up on her bed, crying. She was surrounded by used tissues and holding the goodbye note Alex had left her on the kitchen table. She ignored the accumulating messages from Babs on the answer machine demanding she turn up for work and pressed a button on her iPod so that it played 'Jolene' on repeat. Finally as night fell, a message on her answerphone brought hope - Babs had rung Alex and he had agreed to meet Rinky at the salon the following morning to talk things through.

§

Friday 10.15am. Grace, Theresa and Martina got out of the car, leaving young Alison waiting behind the wheel. All of them were dressed in dark bulky clothes, Grace walked slightly ahead, on full alert. At the top of the alleyway she stopped and signalled to the others. The three mates pulled stockings over their heads, took the replica guns from inside their jackets and burst into the bank. Theresa blocked the exit, Grace passed a demand note to the cashier and Martina pointed her fake weapon at the gormless manager, while three customers looked on, terrified.

At the end of the alleyway, a very nervous Alison was waiting in the car. She looked at her watch; she had three minutes before they were due back. She quickly got out of the car. Fifty metres away Rinky stepped off the bus; she looked and felt terrible. As the heart-broken hairdresser approached the alleyway she was confronted by three masked figures brandishing guns running towards her. She froze. One of them ripped off their mask and shouted "Alison?!" An apologetic young woman appeared from behind a green car, pulling up her knickers. Another of the robbers removed their stocking, and to Rinky's astonishment it was the pretty waitress from the party. "Shit! She knows me!!!" screamed Grace. Theresa roared, "Get her in the car, quick!!" And before she could object, Rinky was bundled into the car by Martina, the gang jumped in either side of her, Alison put her foot on the pedal and the Astra sped away to the sound of a distant police siren.

As the green car turned onto the A127, Rinky was in shock. Grace was trying to soothe her, while a furious Theresa repeatedly hit the back of the driver's seat. "Where the fuck were you?! How comes you weren't in the car?" Alison started crying, and Martina stepped in to defend her friend. By the time they were on the M25 the shouting had stopped but there was tension hanging in the air. What were they going to do with their unexpected hostage? Rinky was looking out of the window imagining that as soon as Alex realised she hadn't turned up he would get in his car and rescue her like a knight in shining armour.

§

Alex was in Curl Up and Dye, eyes closed, moaning with pleasure. A resentful Babs was washing his highlighted foppish hair, determined to keep him there until the very late Rinky turned up. Two more hours passed, there was still no sign of Rinky, and Babs had become a ball of anger. Alex meanwhile had very clean hair.

§

The gang arrived at the secluded cottage around dusk. They all clambered out of the vehicle except for Rinky who was locked inside by Theresa. Grace was about to object when she noticed the vein in Theresa's temple throbbing. She knew this was a danger sign, Theresa was spoiling for a fight, so Grace linked arms with her ex and encouraged her inside, glancing back at the hairdresser, trying to reassure her with a look.

Inside, the cottage was beautifully old fashioned with stone walls and open fireplaces. Unzipping the bag, Theresa looked like the cat with the cream. She filled her pockets, socks, the holes in her ripped jeans with wads of money. Martina and Alison joined in, parading up and down as if they were on a catwalk. Grace appeared from the hallway announcing there was no TV, phone or internet. When she caught sight of them, they all laughed, finally releasing the tension. They sprawled on the sofas, relieved that they'd done it; they'd got the money for Jimmy, they'd got away, and all that was left was to sit it out, wait for the trail to go cold. The congratulatory conversation was interrupted by a loud car horn beeping. Grace ran out of the house and saw Rinky knocking the horn with her head.

After a chilli con carne dinner had been devoured by the gang in the kitchen, Grace suggested they go and count the money. Theresa, Martina and Alison raced to the front room, while Grace quietly shut the kitchen door. "Are you hungry?" Rinky nodded. "Promise not to scream?" Rinky nodded. Grace untied the gag and gave her captive some water. She pulled a chair next to Rinky and tenderly took a stray hair from Rinky's mouth. As she spoon-fed the hungry hostage she whispered, "I'm sorry you got caught up in this. It was supposed to be a victimless crime." Rinky spoke with a croaky voice. "You frightened people in the bank, you frightened me."

"I wish I could put it right, I wish I could turn back time."

"Cher."

"Sorry?"

"If I could turn back time. Released by Cher in 1989."

"You have really terrible taste in music!" Grace and Rinky smiled at each other. Grace continued, "I promise I will think of something. You will be ok."

Although Rinky believed Grace didn't wish her any harm, no amount of kindness, or being spoon-fed a chilli by a gorgeous lesbian, was going to make up for the fact she didn't get to see Alex at Curl Up and Dye.

Later that night Grace and Theresa were sitting on the bed drinking beers, trying to figure out how to resolve 'the problem'. Theresa suggested dumping her body in a river. Grace was outraged. Theresa looked at her ex-girlfriend, not sure why her 'joke' was taken seriously, and then she guessed. "Fuck me, you fancy her!" Grace denied it and hit Theresa with a pillow. During the diverting pillow fight, Grace realised there was no putting the genie back in the bottle, she was falling for their hostage, and even more shocking, she was falling for a Dolly Parton fan.

Rinky was tied to a chair in the dark kitchen: cold, unhappy and without a plan. At 4.49am Rinky suddenly remembered she had a mobile phone in her pocket. She pulled at the socks on her wrists once more, and this time, because she had managed to silence the panicked voices in her head, she found a little leverage on her left side. With slow, patient and dexterous manoeuvrings the hairdresser finally managed to release one hand. She pulled off the gag and pulled out her phone.

Babs was in a deep sleep when her bedside phone rung. She answered it sleepily and was annoyed – it was only Rinky, and she was crying again. She looked at the clock. "Do you know what time it is? Stop crying, I can't understand you...Help?! You've got to help yourself, Rinky!" Babs put down the phone, pulled the plug from the wall and returned to the land of nod.

Rinky's second call was to Alex but to her horror it was answered by a female voice. "Who is this?! I want to speak to Alex!" In her upset Rinky had forgotten to whisper and her voice had woken Theresa. Quick as a flash, Theresa was in the kitchen grabbing the mobile from Rinky's hand and shouting to the others. "What's wrong? What's all the noise?" demanded Grace as she entered the kitchen, quickly followed by a sleepy Martina and Alison. Theresa started to explain the danger when Rinky's mobile rang. They looked at it, unsure what to do. Martina picked it up. "...Who am I? Who the fuck are you?...Ok, ok, I'll tell her. Wanker!"

Martina switched off the phone and looked at the hostage tied to the chair. "Alex says to tell you to stop calling him and that he wants the house back." Rinky bowed her blonde head. Grace could see Theresa was volatile, so she suggested they have a meeting in the morning. Theresa stormed out of the kitchen and the young ones followed. Grace and Rinky were alone again but this time they didn't speak. Grace gently re-tied Rinky's hand to the chair, re-fitted the gag and left the room, ashamed. This was definitely not a victimless crime.

Before the council of war the following morning, things had got worse. Grace had phoned Jimmy; he was very agitated that they had changed the plan. "Who was the look-out? The robbery was on the local news; they showed a photo-fit picture!"

Huddled around a mobile phone, the gang watched the news on the internet with horror and nervous laughter. A witness had seen a blonde woman with a large bag, possibly full of the bank's money, get in a car with several people holding guns, and speed away from the scene of the crime. The photo-fit picture of the look-out was the spitting image of their hostage. Theresa was first on her feet. She put some music on the old record player and pointed the speaker towards the kitchen door.

She spoke quietly but with purpose. "I reckon we drive her into the middle of the mountains in the middle of the night and leave her there. Or better still push her off a cliff. I'm serious, Gracey. There are no other options. We will end up in jail and Jimmy won't have the money for the clinic. Jimmy will die, is that what you want?" Silence, no-one spoke. Theresa suggesting murder and it not being a joke was no joke. Alison looked upset, whispered she hadn't signed up for this. A very worried Grace suggested that they take a few days to weigh everything up. A raise of hands showed Theresa was out-voted for now. Grace still didn't have an answer but she had bought herself, and Rinky, a little more time.

The next few days were surprisingly fun and uncomplicated. Such was the relief that everything was on hold that the gang allowed Rinky to walk around the cottage as long as someone stayed with her and the doors were locked. Rinky, with her new found relative freedom, began to believe there might be an end in sight to the nightmare. She knew making friends with her captors was a good thing to do, firstly because that had been a plot in a *Law and Order* episode she'd enjoyed, and secondly because Rinky was a people person and making everybody happy was what she was good at.

So she offered to cut everyone's hair, and 'Ricky Dinky's' hair salon was set up in the garden. All were thrilled at the pampering and preening, especially Grace who had her hair washed and cut twice in one day. The following day they had a fancy dress party using anything in Aunt Sandy's cottage. Rinky had saved some of the hair she'd cut from the gang and with some tape made herself a moustache and line-danced, which had everyone in stitches. The following day, Grace found an old Dolly Parton album in Aunt Sandy's collection. She waited until the others were out and played the LP at full volume for her delighted guest who sang along to all the tracks. When *9 to 5* came on, the two women danced wildly.

But early the next morning the gloom re-ascended; decision time had arrived. Theresa's proposal was death by rat poison in egg mayonnaise sandwiches. Grace point blank refused to take part when the others drew straws. Alison began to cry: she had pulled out the short one. A picnic was arranged, Martina offered to help Alison prepare the deadly tuck, Theresa was hyped up and an oblivious Rinky was excited at the prospect of an outing.

Rinky had insisted on packing a table cloth. She set it down and unpacked the basket. Theresa picked up the plate of egg mayonnaise sandwiches and offered the poisoned ones without the crusts to Rinky who thanked her and took one. The young ones shook their heads when Theresa offered them the plate, so she made a point of taking one herself (with the crust) and eating it. Rinky smiled. "I have an announcement. I've got a plan that could solve this whole mess." Theresa sneered, called her a nutter and encouraged Rinky to eat up.

"You've got to give the money back. No money missing means no crime and therefore no-one to put in prison. Not you, not Jimmy and not me. It's the right thing to do." Grace wasn't sure she was right in a legal sense but it might at least stop the police pursuing the matter. Theresa was adamant: they had risked everything and Jimmy's life was at stake. She absentmindedly took another sandwich and crammed it in her mouth.

Rinky, still holding one of the poisoned sandwiches, pointed out that Theresa would have to find another way to pay back the five grand she owed the bookies. "How much?" shouted Grace. Theresa's reply was to be violently sick. Alison looked at the plate of sandwiches and screamed. Rinky put her arm around the young woman, comforting her. "It's not your fault, Ali. Eggs can be very tricky."

Twenty minutes later, Theresa was still lying on the floor clutching her stomach but she managed to quietly instruct Grace that it was time for Plan B. "You have to stay here with Rinky, get her drunk, take her for a walk near a cliff. She trusts you. Don't come back til it's done, Gracey. Think of Jimmy. We'll leave you the bike." And then Theresa puked again.

Rinky was standing on a rock, high up in the hills overlooking a valley. She accepted the wine bottle from Grace, took a large swig and laughed. "Are you trying to get me drunk?"

"Do you want me to get you drunk?" Rinky took another swig and then planted a kiss on Grace's mouth. The hairdresser was embarrassed, happy, intoxicated with the wine and the company. She spread her arms out wide and ran along the cliff's edge, enjoying the feeling of freedom. Grace watched her, delighted to see Rinky looking so happy, delighted to taste her on her mouth. But she suddenly remembered Plan B and let out a scream.

Rinky jumped. "You scared me! I nearly fell!" Grace was rooted to the spot. Rinky was very close to the edge. Rinky shouted, "I dare you to take your top off!" and was shocked to see Grace grant her request. Rinky felt unsure what to do. She called out, "Do you want to kiss me?"

"Do you want me to kiss you?" They smiled at each other. Rinky took a deep breath, and ran towards Grace, pulling off her own top. They kissed and the whole world span around them.

Skinny dipping in a deserted Lake Windermere was quickly followed by love-making on the grass banks. Kissing breasts, biting necks, licking, touching and fucking. The two women devoured each other's bodies and embraced each other's hearts.

Until, that is, Grace confessed to Rinky about Plan B. Rinky pulled away from her lover's arms and made her explain the details. Grace was profusely apologetic, reiterating that she had no intention of pushing Rinky off the cliff, but stressed that Theresa was deadly serious, so going back to the cottage was not an option. Rinky grabbed her clothes and stormed off. Grace quickly got dressed and watched as a naked Rinky furiously roared obscenities as she receded into the distance. Eventually Rinky was exhausted. She dressed, marched over to Grace and demanded they do everything exactly as she said. Grace immediately agreed, leaned in for a kiss to check she hadn't completely blown it and was relieved and thrilled with Rinky's passionate reply. As the two of them climbed onto the bike and began to pedal fast Rinky had an epiphany. "I must tell Babs she was right: anger can be a galvanising energy."

They entered the cottage by the back door. Rinky whispered instructions to Alison and Martina, who were very relieved to see them both alive. They quickly and quietly crept to their bedroom to collect their belongings. Grace tiptoed past Theresa, who was snoozing on the sofa with a bucket next to her, to retrieve the all-important money from their room. They loaded the car, jumped in and sped off towards London.

Belting down the M6, Rinky went over her plan in fine detail; there was no room for mistakes. Everyone was keen to follow orders, relieved to be sorting out the nightmare and returning to the relative sanity of home. After Grace had spoken to Jimmy, and Rinky had arranged matters with Babs, Martina asked her older sister what had happened on the mountain. "You both seem so different."

"Your sister seduced me!" teased Rinky.

"I didn't have a choice," replied Grace. "It was that or push you over a cliff!" Alison and Martina whooped and cheered as the new lovers snogged in the back seat of the green Vauxhall Astra (as all young lovers should do).

Stealing Alex's BMW was part expediency and part revenge. Alison didn't want her mum's car involved any further, so following Rinky's suggestion she phoned her mum and told her to report the Astra stolen. They parked outside Rinky's house. Alex would be at the gym this time on a Saturday, but Rinky was surprised to feel a pang of sadness when she walked through the hallway. Luckily she remembered Babs' advice about righteous anger. She grabbed the car keys from the hook, flipped the bird as she came out of the front door and ran back to the others giggling with delight.

§

The nurse at Basildon hospital strong advised Jimmy not to discharge himself but he just gave her a thank you kiss on the cheek. Grace and Martina helped their weak but happy friend to Alex's car waiting for them at the exit. From there, Rinky instructed Alison to drive to Curl Up and Dye where Babs, as agreed, had closed the shop for the afternoon.

Babs, with a fag on the go, had five blonde wigs on blocks. Rinky started snipping and Babs swooped in with the curling tongs. Alison was applying thick make-up on Martina and Jimmy, and all of them were pin-curled in preparation for the wigs. A tap on the door;

everyone on alert. Rinky checked through the blind, smiled and opened the door to Grace. They kissed on the lips, causing a raised eyebrow from Babs, and Grace announced she had found all the outfits. Babs was grinning. "I can't believe you're going to be on the *X Factor*, Rinky. So exciting. Will you give us a mention?" Rinky felt terrible for lying to Babs but knew it was best not to incriminate her nearest and dearest.

§

Five Dolly Parton's in a BMW pull up at the end of the alleyway where 10 days earlier the hairdresser was kidnapped. The blondes are getting out of the car when Jimmy has a bad coughing fit. "Sorry sweetheart, I just can't do it." Grace helps him back inside the car and promises to be back in five minutes.

It's Saturday, 3.18pm, and four Dolly Partons have entered the bank. Chen the security guard, on red alert, immediately gets up out of his seat, and there is a flurry of blonde wigs, confused customers, surprised bank tellers and a stunned manager. One of the Dollys makes an announcement. "Hi, we're from the local college and it's our rag week. We are collecting for Cancer Research." Two of the Dollys hold up buckets for donations, the CD player is turned on, it plays *Jolene* and the four blondes start dancing. Everyone in the bank is laughing, clapping along, and during the routine two Dollys surreptitiously return the bags of stolen money behind the security guard's desk. Minutes later, four Dolly Partons are running down the alleyway.

The gang, half Dolly Parton, half back in their own clothing, are bombing down the motorway. *Jolene* is playing loudly on the CD, everyone singing along. Above the music Grace shouts, "What's the plan now, Rinky?"

Rinky takes a wad of notes from her cleavage. "We need to get Jimmy to the States!" Everyone screams and cheers.

Later that evening Babs almost chokes on her oxtail soup as she watches the Six O'Clock News: "... This afternoon, four thieves in blonde wigs returned two hundred and fifty thousand pounds stolen from the Santander Building Society in Basildon. A note was left by the robbers saying: "The Dolly Parton Fan Club deny any connection."

###

ANGELA CLERKIN is a writer and actor. She has short stories published in *Men & Women* and *East* (Limehouse books). Her Play *Bem-Vindo Estranho* is touring Brazil 2013-15 with the queen of soaps, Regina Duarte. Angela co-wrote *The Bear* with Lee Simpson from Improbable which toured the UK and is currently writing *The Secret Keeper*, supported by the National Theatre Studio. As an actor she has performed in most UK theatres, New York and Sydney Opera House. TV includes *EastEnders*, *Holby*, *Dalziel & Pascoe*, *Sugar Rush* and *The Office*. She has 99 medals for Irish dancing and currently lives with her girlfriend in Greenwich.

FRINGE BENEFITS
HP Munro

SHE STOPPED in surprise at the sheer number of people packed into the confines of the Royal Mile. A riot of colours and sounds converged in the oldest part of Edinburgh. A bagpiper, resplendent in his kilted regalia, stood stock-still, as tourists waited patiently for their turn to stand beside him and get their photo taken. Holly winced as she drew closer. In her years in the British Army the sound of the pipes was a familiar, if noisy, reminder of serving alongside The SCOTS. She recalled reading somewhere that the pipes were originally used to scare the enemy – a purpose she assumed that had served them well.

The swirls of the bagpipes fought for their place amongst the other sounds on the section of the street cordoned off to traffic. Walking on, she became aware of a street performer's voice, amplified through a small PA system and battling to be heard over a string quartet; their being but ten feet from a man playing his guitar and singing about how *everybody hurts*.

Further on still, a small stage held a youth group performing a medley of songs from their show in the hope of selling more tickets. Adding a final layer to the rich tapestry of aural stimulation, and underpinning the cacophony, was the unique sound of an Indian sitar, wafting over the heads of those thronging the area.

She stepped into the crowd ready to experience all that the Edinburgh Fringe had to offer and had moved only a few feet when a leaflet promoting a show was thrust into her hand. She gave it a cursory glance and intended to deposit it in the nearest bin when she had a chance. Ten further steps and she had collected six more.

Eight. Nine. Ten. She had to admire the energies of the marketers, though found herself reflecting on the carbon footprint of each step she'd taken, observing with irony the *'recycle'* symbol on all of the promotionals she was holding. Pushing the leaflets into a waste bin, she continued to weave her way down the narrow street until she managed to find a bit of space in Parliament Square: a welcome space adjacent to St Giles' Cathedral.

She squinted up at the crown-like dome of the cathedral and stopped to observe as tourists and locals alike paused at a specific area on the cobbled street outside the cathedral and spat onto it. As she drew closer, she saw that the cobbles were arranged into a heart-shaped pattern, with a circle in the centre and the tell-tale remains of people's saliva visible in the centre. She wondered what custom she had witnessed and resolved to buy a guidebook. Climbing over the calf-height black chains that demarked the square from the street, she entered into the melee again.

Within moments, her attention was caught by a crowd of people clearly transfixed by a street performer. Standing at the back of the crowd, she was enjoying the gasps of those with an evidently better viewing position, as flaming torches and swords were tossed into the air, when she heard an alarmed cry.

"Stop! Thief!"

She turned quickly, her body flooding with adrenaline. There was a blur of activity as people immediately behind her moved out of the way of a running figure. As a serving soldier, Holly understood the innate response of fight, or flight. The one she struggled with was stand, stare and do nothing.

She twisted as the figure came within striking distance. Instinctively, she extended her right arm and caught the fleeing man around the throat. His head snapped back at the contact, and at the same moment she deftly swept her left leg round, taking his legs out from under him.

Landing heavily on the cobbled road, the air was knocked out of his lungs upon impact and he immediately started to cough and clutch at his throat – precisely where Holly's forearm had made contact.

It was only at that moment, when Holly looked down, that she noticed that the man she had incapacitated was dressed in a black and white striped top and black trousers. He had a black eye-mask painted onto his face, and at his side was a brown sack marked 'swag'. Her eyes widened, as the realisation hit her that she may have made a rather spectacular error of judgment.

As the man lay on the ground, his eyes looked at her accusatorily as he tried valiantly to regain his breath. Another man, wearing a policeman's uniform and carrying a large brown truncheon, jogged up.

"What the hell happened?" he asked in a clipped English tone, and he looked around at the assembled people for an answer. The man on the ground, with one hand still held at his throat, pointed a finger towards Holly.

"She's what happened," he choked.

"I am so sorry. I heard 'Stop! Thief!', and I reacted," Holly apologised profusely, holding out her hand to help the man up. He slapped her hand away and slowly regained his feet. Holly bent down to collect his 'swag' bag for him and sheepishly held it out. He snatched it with one hand, the other still rubbing his neck gingerly.

"Crazy bitch," he muttered under his breath, nodding to his associate. They shot her a final derisory look before slipping into the crowd.

Holly let out a slow breath and realised a number of people were still watching her carefully. She plastered on a broad smile. "If you enjoyed that performance, come see us at eight pm each night, at the Gilded Balloon," she said confidently, remembering the name of one of the venues from the earlier leaflets.

"Do you have a leaflet?" a man asked.

She looked at him, with her eyebrows furrowed in earnest. "No, I'm all out. Sorry."

He nodded and moved on, though not before casting her a rather dissatisfied backward glance. As the small group of spectators dispersed, Holly dropped her head and shook it, chuckling to herself. When she looked up, she was surprised to see two blue eyes regarding her with amusement.

"You know, if you wanted to kill a street performer I'd have gone with the sitar player," the owner of the blue eyes said with a smile, as she took a couple of steps towards Holly.

Holly turned towards where the man sat cross-legged, his back against a building while he continued to play, ignoring both the winces on the faces as people walked by and the lack of coins on the black cloth set out in front of him.

Holly cocked her head, and her eyes scanned the area around him as she calculated how best – in combative theory – to get close enough to apply pressure to his carotid artery: perhaps not enough to kill him, but enough for him to at least lose consciousness for a while and give those in the vicinity blessed relief from his playing.

"Are you working out how you would do it?" the woman whispered, looking between Holly and the sitar player.

"I don't know, that depends. Did you just take a hit out on an innocent street performer?" Holly asked evenly, before smiling as the other woman laughed.

"His playing is bad, but I'll let him live," she responded.

Holly smirked and pulled a wallet from the pocket of her jeans. Selecting a couple of coins, she walked over towards the sitar player and tossed them onto the cloth in front of him. "It's your lucky day," she murmured, before turning back towards her co-conspirator. "The name's Holly, by the way, Holly Preston," and with Bond-like charisma she extended her right hand, this time in a gesture of friendship and not an attempt at incapacitation.

"Katie Jackson," came the response, in a warm tone.

"I bring coffee," Katie said, holding out a takeaway cup.

Holly looked up from her phone and smiled. "Thanks," she said, taking the cup, as Katie sat down on the small wall beside her in Hunter Square, just behind the Tron Kirk.

After Holly's assault on the street performer and their granting the sitar player a reprieve, they had started chatting. Discovering they were both on their own, they had agreed to experience the rest of the day's available entertainment together.

They had moved to the square to take stock of the options available to them and decide what they both wanted to do and see. Holly looked around, taking in the collection of people sitting in the area. There seemed to be a high number of teenagers in dark t-shirts, with their hair dyed an assortment of shades of red, or black, or both.

"Do you think we're in the goth zone?" she whispered out of the side of her mouth, motioning with her head.

Katie looked up from her guidebook and scrunched up her nose. "It would appear that we're in their natural habitat." She waggled her eyebrows at Holly before returning her attention to her book. "Ah-ha!" she exclaimed, holding the guide book up for Holly to see. "There are a couple of theories as to why you should spit on it. It used to be the site of 'The Old Tollbooth', where people were held before they were hung – often without trial – and where you went to pay your taxes. So it's either to show disdain at the injustice of the hangings or in protest at having to pay tax." She closed the book, looking pleased with herself that she had managed to find the answer to Holly's query regarding the strange custom she'd witnessed earlier.

"Had I known it was a protest at taxes, I'd have peed on it," Holly said against the rim of her coffee cup.

Katie snorted loudly. "Could you make sure I'm not drinking when you make a crack like that," she said, wiping drops of coffee from her chin. "So, if you want a break from here then we can take a walk up to Calton Hill."

Standing, Holly held out her hand to help Katie up. "Ok then, let's get going."

As they climbed up a second set of steep steps, eventually reaching a sloping pathway, Holly's focus was immediately drawn towards an imposing Grecian structure that dominated the skyline on top of the hill ahead of them and overlooking Edinburgh.

"What the hell is that?" she asked.

Katie looked closely at her guidebook and read aloud. "It's the National Monument. Started in 1826 to commemorate the British dead in the Napoleonic Wars, based on the Parthenon in Greece and known as Edinburgh's Disgrace, as it was never finished since they ran out of money."

Holly looked quizzically at her, as she started to giggle.

"I'm sorry, I borrowed this from my friend, and she's written her own commentary in the margins," she explained, waving the book. "She says that nowadays it has some stiff competition from the Scottish Parliament and the Edinburgh Tram Scheme for the title, and at least the Georgians had the good sense to stop when a project went over budget." Katie pulled Holly's arm and began walking up the hill leading on from the steps.

Holly couldn't help but smile, as she allowed herself to be tugged up the steep incline. "They have a cannon?!" she remarked, as she stared up towards the barrel of the gun, sitting proudly on a cobbled area.

"Typical solider – always focusing on the armory," Katie grinned. "Will you take my photo?" she asked, pulling out a small camera from her backpack and holding it out towards Holly.

Holly took the camera and watched in an amused fashion as Katie climbed onto the barrel of the cannon and held her arms out wide, smiling broadly.

"Your turn," she insisted, taking the camera as she climbed off the barrel and pushed Holly towards the aged piece of artillery. Sighing, Holly climbed onto the barrel. The cool of the brass seeped through her jeans as she sat patiently, waiting on Katie to take her photograph. She was about to get down when Katie turned towards a petite woman walking by, accompanied by an equally diminutive black terrier. With an audible thanks, Katie handed the camera over and bounded towards Holly. "She's going to take one of the both of us," she said breathlessly, throwing her leg over the cannon's barrel and positioning herself in front of Holly.

Holly smiled tightly; her thighs were soon pressed against Katie, as she wriggled backwards into position. With her chin almost resting on Katie's shoulder, she was treated to the subtle scent of her perfume each time she breathed. With what might be most accurately described as an intimate distance between them, she felt a long forgotten sensation of her stomach flipping and a large proportion of her blood repositioning itself to where it thought she needed it most.

"Smile!" the woman taking the picture called out cheerfully.

Holly managed to maintain her smile, despite feeling betrayed by her body's intuitive response and subconscious desire. She was supposed to be in Edinburgh recovering from a relationship, not lusting after a woman who, to be fair, seemed perfectly content nestled between her thighs, and grinning for the photograph.

She walked around only half-listening, as Katie pointed out the array of monuments on the hill. Her mind was still distracted by the recent surge of arousal that she had experienced.

"And it drops each day at one o'clock...Are you listening to me?" Katie asked.

"What? Sorry." Holly looked sheepishly at Katie. "My mind went away from me there," she apologised.

"Is it anything I can help with?" Katie asked, her tone full of concern. "I'm a brilliant listener." She smiled with encouragement.

Holly shook her head. "It's nothing,"

"Well, it must be pretty important if you're zoning out while I'm telling you about Nelson's ball!"

"His what?" Holly spluttered.

"Naughty!" Katie laughed, smacking Holly's nose lightly with the guidebook. "His time ball," she clarified, pointing towards the top of the tall tower, which was designed to resemble an upturned telescope.

Holly rolled her eyes, silently vowing to raise her brain from the gutter, where it apparently was resting contentedly. Standing in the shadow of the tower, she looked over the cityscape in front of her and towards a group of hills lying snugly within the urban confines. This wild, and striking, portion of the skyline looked at odds with its city location. "Not content with cannons, they also have mountains in the middle of the city!" she remarked, nodding towards the peaks.

Katie followed her gaze; she dropped her guidebook to her side and smiled. "That's not a mountain! That's Arthur's Seat."

"How big was Arthur?" Holly asked, shielding her eyes from the sun to get a better view of the collection of lolling slopes and rocky outcrops.

Laughing, Katie shook her head. "We can climb it, if you want?"

"Maybe tomorrow," Holly replied absently, being captivated by the view. She was too absorbed in the scenery to notice the smile that crept across Katie's face as she inadvertently made plans for the next day.

"What did you think of the show?" Katie asked, looping her arm through Holly's as they walked in step, leaving the grandness of the Assembly Rooms behind them and heading out into the warm evening sunlight basking George Street.

Holly sucked the inside of her cheek. "Well, let's examine the facts: I've just spent forty minutes watching one man reenact the entire *Lord of the Rings* in Elvish."

"Than'youverymuch," Katie drawled, in a commendable impersonation.

"Wasn't funny the first time," Holly said dryly, ignoring the pout that it generated from Katie.

"Well, I rate it higher than *JFK - The Musical*," Katie sighed, tightening her grip on Holly's arm as she protectively stopped her from stepping out onto the road and into the path of a rather focused cyclist.

"That's not a very high bar to set," Holly laughed, allowing herself to be pulled closer to Katie. With the closeness of their physical proximity more than apparent to her, she told herself that her acceptance of such had nothing, nothing, to do with her mounting attraction. Much in the same way, her mindset had earlier maintained that her placing her lips so close to Katie's ear when wryly commenting on the *'original bravery'* of the show they were watching, which consisted of one man walking over mousetraps, was just to ensure that she could be heard.

As the sun's rays bathed George Street's sandstone façades in a rich amber hue, they reflected that, in the course of day, they had succeeded in their challenge to sample the worst that the festival had to offer. With over three thousand to choose from, ranging in quality from the astoundingly awful to the breathtakingly brilliant, they considered this to be quite an accomplishment.

"So what's next on the agenda?" Holly asked as they crossed the street and started to unconsciously wend their way back towards the Old Town.

As they strolled, dusk started to fall, and Holly's eyes widened in surprise as she spotted the time on one of the four clock faces illuminated at the top of the imposing tower of the iconic Balmoral Hotel.

"It's ten o'clock!" Holly said, in disbelief. "How did that happen?"

"Time flies when you're with a hot woman," Katie said, with mock modesty.

Holly chuckled. "I'm fairly sure that's not how the saying goes."

They walked on in amicable silence, following the route of the black railings that encircled the formal gardens, and dissected the New from the Old in the city.

"Do you want to call it a night?" Holly asked, aware of a heaviness in her chest at the thought that their time together would soon be over. She was still processing her reaction to this sensation when Katie answered.

"Weeeell," Katie said, as she raised her shoulders up towards her ears. "There's a club that I was going to check out, if you're up for that?"

With immediate relief, the heaviness that Holly had experienced on her chest lifted. "Totally up for that!" She blushed as Katie raised an eyebrow and smirked at her rushed response. "I mean, only if you want to," Holly amended, frowning as she felt the heat rise further in her cheeks.

Katie tugged her, closing the distance between them once again, and whispered softly, "I liked the first response better." Before Holly could respond, Katie was looking straight ahead and waving her free arm in the air, singing brightly, "This is the end of our story, ended with a bullet from the book repository."

Holly snorted as Katie sang from the awful JFK musical that they had seen earlier, and at the same time she felt her stomach flip at Katie's whispered comment. "I'm not sure what worries me more," she laughed. "Your singing, or the fact that you remember the words!"

110

"I refuse to be offended by that! Let's go somewhere, and you can buy me a drink."

Holly followed Katie down past the church and the square where they had enjoyed their coffee earlier in the day and noted that Katie walked with purpose down a steep and cobbled wynd running off the Mile. As she walked, Holly could hear music coming from an open doorway near the bottom of the narrow routeway. Katie stopped and turned, holding her arms aloft as if to present the club to Holly as a triumph of discovery.

Outside the doorway, several women stood smoking, their eyes raking over Katie as her hips started to sway to the beat of the music emanating from inside while she waited for Holly to catch up.

As she reached Katie, Holly shot the smokers a proprietorial glare. She surprised herself with the sudden surge of jealousy that their looks had prompted.

"Voila!" Katie said smiling, still swaying to the music and unaware of the appreciative looks that her pert buttocks, enticingly outlined in tight jeans, were getting from the women outside the club. She noticed the disapproval apparent on Holly's face and turned towards where she was looking. Her eyes took in the assembled women. "If you want to go somewhere else?" she added, her voice laced with disappointment.

"What?" Holly tore her eyes from staring down the women and looked at Katie. "No, let's go in." She smiled broadly and reached for Katie's hand. She laced her fingers through Katie's and led her into the club, making sure she gave the smoking women another challenging stare as they walked through the entrance.

"Seriously, if I've read this wrong, and I've made you feel uncomfortable, we can go somewhere else; it's not a problem," Katie said quietly.

Holly noticed that Katie's confident manner, which she had unconsciously felt secure with during their day together, was suddenly absent, as she observed her chewing on her lower lip. She allowed her head to fall to the side as she captured Katie's gaze and gave a small smile. "Here is fine, honestly." She glanced around the dimly lit hallway. "Home from home," she said softly, hoping that Katie picked up on her meaning.

"Youse comin' or goin'?" asked a woman, sitting just inside the entranceway, in a broad – if somewhat ascorbic – Scottish accent. She waved the stamp that she used to mark the hands of those paying their entrance fee.

"We're coming, I mean staying," Holly said, pulling out her wallet and feeling a blush redden her cheeks. "We're staying," she repeated, putting money on the desk and holding her hand out for the smiley purple stamp.

Following on, Katie similarly held her hand out to be duly stamped. Her confident demeanor had returned, and she leaned in conspiratorially towards the doorwoman. "I preferred coming."

The woman laughed, and the indifferent manner of her expression disappeared as her features became animated, and she gave Holly an appraising look. "I don't blame you," she grinned, then turned to the women standing behind Katie. "Next," she shouted, with a smile still dancing on her lips.

Holly rolled her eyes and blew a puff of air up towards her fringe. "Can we go in now?" she asked, almost dragging Katie into the body of the small club.

Katie pulled Holly closer as the music slowed, and neither minded as their sticky skin made contact. They had danced liked demons since their arrival, both using the innocent act as a method of dissipating at least some of the sexual tension that was coursing through their bodies. However, their effort was soon undone, as their bodies pressed against each other on the tightly packed dance floor. Katie looked up and smiled as she looped her arms around Holly's neck. Holly returned the smile, while slipping her arms around Katie's waist.

Their coats, and several other layers, had been long discarded in the hot club, and Katie was now dressed in a white tank top that had ridden up during her earlier energetic dancing. Both felt their pulse quicken as Holly's fingertips found Katie's sweat-soaked back, and their bodies moved in rhythm with the music. Their heads were moving closer to each other. Holly's breathing became shallower, as she moved her gaze from the blue eyes watching her intently to their owner's lips, which were slightly parted and only inches from her own. She was poised to accept their invitation, when bright lights snapped on and a voice came over the speakers asking them if they had 'homes to go to and beds to shag in'. It was only then that both of them realised that the music had stopped sometime before.

Katie licked her lips carefully, while extracting herself reluctantly from Holly's embrace. "Time to go, I suppose," she said, wistfully.

Holly smoothed out her top, trying to regain some composure, "S'pose so."

They were pulling on their coats as they exited the club and entered into the twilight with the other clubbers. Opportunistic taxi drivers were lined up outside, waiting for the club to spill out, in the hope of picking up a fare.

"Cab or walk?" Holly asked. "I should point out, I have no idea how to get to my hotel," she grinned, "therefore, I'm in your hands."

Katie cocked an eyebrow. "Not quite, but you will be soon," she said, as she opened the door to the black cab and let Holly climb in first before getting in and pulling the door closed.

H.P. MUNRO lives in Edinburgh with her wife and a wauzer named Boo. She started writing in 2010 when a new job took her away from home a lot and she found herself in airports, on flights and in hotel rooms with room service for one. The job didn't last but the love of writing did.

Her début novel, *Silver Wings,* won the Golden Crown Literary Society Historical Fiction award in 2014. Her novels *Grace Falls* and *Stars Collide* were published in 2014 and quickly became lesbian romance bestsellers. She is currently working on her fourth novel, *Return to Grace Falls.*

www.red-besom-books.com/

POSTCARDS FROM SPAIN
Nic Herriot

"HE'S A CREDIT to you." That's what Mrs Bartholomew said. She's right you know. Frank always studied, at school he was good at maths, he didn't like sports, he liked sums. "The numbers tell a story," he would say. I'd look at his homework and say that they weren't telling me anything. He went to university for three years and then had to study again. Imagine studying for six years before you qualify. It'll pay off one day he would say. He was right. He and Stephanie have a lovely house now. They have a new conservatory on the back. I had coffee in it once. It's a bit hot in there when the sun shines but it's sure to have increased the value of the house, a good investment. His dad would have been proud of him. He's a good lad that one.

I said to Rachel, "That's what you should be looking for, a husband, someone like Frank. You were at university for more than seven years. I don't understand how you haven't qualified yet. How can you still be training when Frank has a proper job now? I don't see why you didn't marry one of those doctors when you had the chance. You missed a good opportunity to better yourself there you know. Being a doctor is a respected profession."

"Mum," she said in that tone of voice they use when they think they know better than you. "I am training to be a doctor."

Who's going to trust a woman doctor anyway? I didn't say that out loud mind; she would only start.

Frank and Stephanie came over for lunch today. Frank wanted to take me to a restaurant as a treat. I said to him, "Why go out when I can do a lovely roast at home and it won't be a bother?" Afterwards he washed all the dishes, just like he did when he was a boy. Then he sat me down. He thought he would tell me now, he said, so I could get used to it.

"It sounds like you're going to give me bad news," I said. "You're not ill or something are you?" He wasn't ill, but it was bad news. He wouldn't be home for Christmas. He said he knew it would upset me, but he has to work away this year. He has been given an important role with the company in Spain. He knew it wouldn't be the same, not being at home, but he had to take this "opportunity of a life time".

"Stephanie and I will be home next year... maybe."

Yes, I'm disappointed. I told him that I was proud of him and that he must go if that's where the company thinks he should be.

Stephanie mentioned that they had dinner with Rachel and her friend, Joanne, last night, and they had already told Rachel about the job. I said to Stephanie that she should be careful. I think the only reason Joanne hangs around with Rachel is because she might be after Frank. He is a good catch what with his promotion and new job in Spain. Frank and Stephanie laughed and Frank said, "You are daft." I don't know what they were laughing about; I'm not being silly. Joanne got herself invited to their wedding you know. Even knowing he's married she could still be after Frank. There are women out there like that. Gold diggers we called them when I was young.

"Anyway, back to you two, I thought the Spanish were Catholic. Wouldn't they have a holiday at Christmas? You can come back then."

He said, "You really are daft, Mum. I'm not Catholic so I'll be working. Someone has to work, otherwise the financial world crumbles. The Americans will still be working, not to mention the Japanese: they don't celebrate Christmas. You can spend Christmas with Rachel and Joanne. They would love to have you."

"I think Joanne will want to spend Christmas with her family, don't you?" I wasn't happy. It seems as if they have been talking about going to Spain for a while... don't know why they couldn't have told me earlier. And I am a little upset they told Rachel first.

He caught that habit from Dad you know: calling me daft.

"Frank seems happy in Spain." Mrs Bartholomew and I were sitting in the new café that has just opened up on Market Street. The prices are a bit high but at least you can get waitress service... if you can call it that. The young girls, what do they know about service these days?

I told her all about how Frank had been headhunted for the job. "That's the modern term," I said, "headhunted."

"Sounds violent," said Mrs Bartholomew.

"Yes, but these days it means that another company wants Frank to work for them, because he is very good at his job."

And she said, "But didn't you say that he is being transferred? You can't be headhunted within the same company can you?"

"Now you're complicating things," I said. "Frank says he was headhunted and I don't know enough about the business world to know anything different. If their father were here I'm sure he would've explained it to me. Anyway, it was worth the effort he put in, going to university and then all that studying afterwards. He is a chartered accountant you know. I'm very proud of the boy."

"What's the difference between an accountant and a chartered accountant then?" I do like Mrs Bartholomew, but she does go on a bit.

"I have no idea," I said. Frank did explain it once but I couldn't see the difference. ''Think of it this way," he said. "Stephanie has a new kitchen already and I've only been working with the company for a year." That's why he's in Spain at the moment...

"Headhunted."

"Yes, headhunted...his company has a branch out there. That's why he can't be home for Christmas; there's a lot of work to do in this new branch."

Sometimes people can make it such hard work when you're trying to tell them good news.

Rachel phoned me this evening. She wanted to check I was all right, what with Frank having been away for a month already. Why wouldn't I be all right? It will do Frank's career good. He is responsible for an entire branch now and Rachel said, "I know you wanted Frank to stay with you for Christmas but as he's away you could come over and spend Christmas with us."

I said, "It's only right you should come home and have Christmas with me. After all, you are family. It's what Dad would have wanted."

Apparently, although she has Christmas Day off she is due back in casualty that evening. It would be easier for her if I came over to her house. She would pick me up and I could stay until Boxing Day.... or longer if I wanted.

I told her, "I don't understand why you have to work anyway. I thought the whole point of going to that medical college was to meet a young doctor so you didn't have to work. After all," I said, "Stephanie doesn't need to work."

She said in that tone, "Mum... don't start." I don't know what she means by that. I wasn't starting anything. I just don't see the point in her being in debt with all that studying.

"And anyway, they don't trust women doctors," I said.

"Who are *they*?" she asked.

"Well," I said. "Now you're just being clever. I have to go; there is someone at the door."

There wasn't. Anyone at the door that is. She thinks I'm deaf, but I heard that other woman in the room. I think that if Rachel didn't work so hard she could decorate that sitting room of hers, and it could be a really lovely place.

I had a postcard from Frank. It looks lovely out there, although too hot for me. I don't know how Stephanie copes with the heat. They are fine, he says. He's working hard and Stephanie is sunbathing and relaxing.

As I was in town this morning, I called in on Mrs Bartholomew. She has one of those new bungalows the Association has built near the park. Her daughter has invited her to have Christmas dinner with them, in a restaurant. Mrs Bartholomew says her daughter won't have to do all the work that goes into it. All the vegetables that need peeling, missing out on watching the children opening their presents. Having dinner in a restaurant means she can enjoy the whole day without any work, so more time to play with the children. I said it wouldn't be the same, not like being at home for dinner, the smell of the turkey, the left-overs for tea.

She interrupted with, "The piles of washing up." I ignored her. I said that I was still hoping that Frank could come home just for the weekend. I'm sure he would try; he knows how important Christmas is. All the family together.

She said, "You should spend the day with Rachel and Joanne. You know Rachel wants you to go over to hers. Joanne is a nice young woman; you'll have a good time. Rachel is your family as well." She said that she'd bumped into them in Morrisons the other day. I said that Morrisons is nothing like it was in the old days and she agreed. Nothing was as good as it was in the old days. "Anyway," she said, "they were out shopping together, and they looked very happy."

That girl seems to go everywhere with Rachel. She should see some of her other friends. If she would just go on one date with a nice young doctor...I wonder if that new doctor in my surgery is single. What's his name now? Dr Sullivan or something. Now he would be a good catch. Not that her training would go to waste; at least she would know what he was talking about.

I had visitors this afternoon. The police. They were looking for Frank. They want him to "help with their enquiries."

I told them, "He's away at the moment. He is working abroad. I don't know how he can help you." One of them walked across from the sofa and picked up Frank's postcard and read it.

"So, Frank's in Spain now is he?"

"Yes," I said. "He moved out there a couple of months ago. He has a very important job."

"Do you have his address?"

"No, he is still looking for the best area to suit his position. He hasn't decided where he's going to live yet. When he does he will let me know."

"Can I take this?" he asked, showing me the card. I was about to say no, but he was already putting it in his pocket. The young constable gave me a receipt so I could get it back later.

"Thank you for your time," he said. "We will see ourselves out." Just like that.

It was really busy today. Rachel and her friend called round this afternoon. The police had been to ask them about Frank.

"It sounds like he's involved in something illegal: embezzling or something similar. I wonder what sort of company he's really working for." That was Joanne; what does she know?

"Are you accusing Frank of being a criminal?"

"Mum," said Rachel in that tone again. "Joanne is a barrister; she deals with this sort of thing all the time."

"Well, I don't need her coming into my house making things out of nothing about Frank."

"Mum," said Rachel. "We don't want a fight; I just wanted to make sure you are ok after their visit. Let's change the subject. Have you thought about Christmas yet? It's only a few weeks away. Do you want to come to ours?"

"*Ours*?" I said. "Doesn't Joanne want to go and stay with her family?"

"I'm Joanne's family," said Rachel. "I think it's time we went anyway. I'll call round next week after my early shift."

As I opened the door, I said, "Your Dad would want you to come home for Christmas you know. To have it here, like the old days."

"Yes Mum." And she kissed me goodbye.

Now that Frank's in Spain I watch the weather forecast on the BBC to see what it's like over there. They're having a hard time of it. "Unseasonable frosts and snow on the south coast," the girl said. "It might affect the winter tourists who are expecting warm sunshine."

The police were here again this morning. The same detective. With a different police officer this time. It seems Frank's not in Spain.

"It was a false trail." He was apparently just passing through on his way to another country. The detective thinks Frank might be on his way to South America.

"Do you know where he is?"

I was indignant. "No I don't. If Frank told me he was in Spain that's where he is. He doesn't need to lie to me."

He gave me my postcard; I put it back in its place on the mantelpiece.

"Well," he said walking to the door, "if you hear from him you will let me know won't you?" I didn't say anything. I held the door open for them to leave.

I didn't show them Frank's latest one. It arrived yesterday. From Spain. Well I haven't had time to read it properly, and I didn't want him taking it away. It seems as if they are still enjoying themselves out there and Stephanie is getting a lovely tan sunbathing on the beach.

Rachel phoned me this evening. The police had been in touch with her as well. It looks like Frank is in serious trouble, especially if they are now looking for him in America. She wanted to know if I had decided to come over to theirs for Christmas dinner, now that Frank wouldn't be coming home.

I said, "I don't know why things have to change. Dad would have wanted you to come home for Christmas, especially with Frank being away." There was a silence down the phone. Then she said, "Will you stop talking as if Dad is dead. I visit him every summer in Brighton. Who do you think gave Frank and myself the funds to get through university?"

Why is it that daughters can be so hurtful? Why would she say something like that? "Mum," she said. "Please... I don't want to lose you, but you have to move on. You have to realise that the past is the past. Not everyone is perfect. It would be really lovely to have you for Christmas dinner... with Joanne and me. I know it won't be with Frank and Stephanie but you will be with family... you will be with me... your daughter."

It's Christmas in three days' time. Mrs Bartholomew called round this morning. I gave her a lovely Christmas card. Marks and Spencer's do a lovely set. A pack of six robins for £3.20. It seems that Rachel has been to see her, so she knows all about Frank and the trouble with the police. Why does that girl have to tell everyone about our business? It seems the police are looking for a lot of people. Frank is working for a dry cleaning company. He is not in finance. Apparently it was his job to launder the money the company made. That's why he had to leave the country at short notice. Well, that's what Mrs Bartholomew said. I do wonder about her sometimes. I can see her moving to that care home up the road any day soon. She asked me if I had decided what I was doing for Christmas. I told her that I would be going to stay with Rachel and her friend. Mrs Bartholomew said well done. She had been hoping I would finally see sense and go.

"You should be proud of Rachel; she is doing really well at the hospital, and Joanne is a lovely young woman. It is always good to spend Christmas with family."

"Well," I said. "I'm only going for the day, until Rachel starts her shift. I want to be home for when Frank phones me, to wish me a merry Christmas."

NIC HERRIOT After years of inflicting her writing on her work colleagues in the in-house magazine, Nic Herriot finally let loose her creativity in 1995 when she completed an MA in Creative Writing at Trinity Carmarthen. Her ideas come from family, friends and adventures that happen in the real world. All her family have left home to save themselves the embarrassment except her poor wife, who is waiting for her passport to come through. She has a couple of stories published and really enjoys the performance side of reading her work in public.

THE BUTTERFLY COLLECTOR
Karen Campbell

I HAD A BROKEN heart and felt sorry for myself. The bubble of fragile love that I had wrapped around me had not taken a lot to pop. A dose of infidelity had hastened my plastic love to the recycling bin and sent a flurry of tears to blur my eyes. The same old clichés rolled off my tongue, as I cradled a bottle of wine and the t-shirt my philandering ex had slept in.

I could still smell her night-time scents, with their whispers of broken promises. I could not throw away her t-shirt just yet but perhaps I could stop hurling my heart under stampeding feet.

In a sea of faces, I have never met eyes with a soul mate and what is the point of having a soul if you never find its mate?

After yet another night of silence in my flat, the clock ticking louder and louder, I decided I would have to get away. A woman at work knew someone, who knew someone else who had a holiday cottage at the coast to rent out over the summer. It sounded perfect for me: I could swim every day, take long walks on the beach and 'find myself'.

I got her number and 'found myself' agreeing to an extended stay of four weeks, starting almost as soon as the school I taught in broke up for the summer. It was something to aim towards, crossing each day off my calendar with a building excitement. Everywhere I looked in my flat reminded me of 'the ex'. I could not bring myself to say her name any longer. I was single now, bleeding on my own. Walking past lovers kissing reminded me of her stolen kisses behind my back.

My friends asked me: "What heals a broken heart?"

"Solitude, time and determination to forget," I would have said but I was wrong. Only one thing heals a broken heart and that is love, but love is not for the faint-hearted. Love is a butterfly explosion that splinters the soul.

So, I was still a right misery guts when the morning came that I would arrive at my holiday cottage. The landlady had said there would be a key under an ornament at the door that looked like a mushroom, as she was going on holiday and could not be there to welcome me. She had also mentioned that, as it was a three-bedroomed cottage, I might have to share, depending on her bookings. I had agreed to that at the time of our telephone conversation but as I approached the house in my car, singing loudly to 'Biffy Clyro', I felt the quiet beauty silence any misgivings I'd had about this break. It was perfect in its solitude and I really didn't want to have to share. Four weeks of being on my own would erase the hurt of being cheated on and let me build myself back up.

If I could not learn to live with myself and my many faults, what chance would someone else have with me? I don't generally like being on my own, I prefer to be part of a couple. I like going to sleep knowing that I will wake up beside another woman. I like to be surprised by the way love will run up my windpipe and strangle my breath. I don't like being surprised by my girlfriend sleeping with my best friend in my bed.

But, I would rather be alone than be taken for granted. That's a slow drip of unhappiness that drowns a relationship, and I would always rather swim away to the miles of ocean in front, not knowing what lay ahead, than turn back to what had been behind. We walk forward in life for a reason.

Pulling into the gravel-lined drive leading up to the cottage, idyllic in its ivy-covered armour, I noticed there were no other cars parked out front and my hopes were raised to the idea I had this beautiful house to myself for four weeks. I could already hear the laps of the sea tides as I stepped out my motor, feeling the crunch of pebbles under my feet and I licked my lips to taste the salt in the air. Too many times it had been the salt of tears I had been tasting. No more, I vowed, stepping forward to look for a mushroom with a key hidden below.

I found it sitting on the top step to the front door, welcoming me with its bright red. I lifted it up and found a key, as the owner had promised. I stood for a second with my hand poised on the key in the lock, ready to turn.

"Everything changes now," a voice within told me. "What you thought was real will fade and what you thought faded will become real."

It was not a moment for the faint-hearted. Like love isn't. I have a heart made of steel but the women I've chosen are acid-love. I know that I have been worn down but that ends now, as the lock turns and the door opens. Today begins the new me, without someone else to define me.

As I walked up the staircase that opened into the sitting-room, I caught myself smiling. Already I felt a tiny bit better. Just getting away from the circle that held all the hurt in my life felt liberating, like throwing off a coat made heavy by a bitter rain. I was lighter as I skipped up the stairs, seeing the bedroom doors and not knowing which one was mine.

I looked at the keys in my hand and saw I had bedroom one. It was simplistic and perfect, clean and warm. I dropped my bag and went to open the window, immediately grateful for the shore view I had. I inhaled deeply and smiled again. This was going to be a great holiday.

I woke up from my afternoon nap, disorientated, with a gentle breeze brushing my face and the cawing of the gulls calling to my ears. It took me a moment to realise where I was: at the place where my heart would be healed, and a small smile grew.

I leapt from the bed, not knowing I was full of hope for my future, just knowing that this house was going to be good for me.

There was no television or radio to distract me and it was a welcome relief when I saw I had no signal on my mobile phone. There were well-stocked bookshelves that could keep me occupied on a night, after relaxing days of sunshine and swimming.

I fell straight asleep that first night, with my window open and the moonlight illuminating a trail on the water. I would walk in the moon trail tomorrow.

The next morning, I made a light breakfast and before long found myself sunbathing on the sand. The heat sapped my energy and I lay soaking up the rays for a while until I forced myself to go for a swim.

Walking back to the cottage later, it struck me that I hadn't once thought of my ex. I was having a little self-congratulatory moment when I saw the back of a woman standing at the kitchen sink. She must be a new guest, arriving today while I had been out.

I caught myself checking her out, which could not be helped as she had cut-off jeans on that barely covered her bum cheeks at the top of her long, creamy legs. My hungry eyes devoured them.

I coughed to get her attention and she turned, flashing me a brilliant smile, strangling my breath. Her blonde, wavy hair bounced off her shoulders and her skin glowed. I became a jellyfish. I felt my jaw slacken, as I stared at her ocean blue eyes, because I had never believed in love at first sight.

"I'm Perry," she said. I felt an electricity tingle over me at the sound of her voice.

"I'm Rosie. Have you just arrived?" I asked.

"No," she said. "I've been here for a while."

I didn't know quite what to say, so I made my excuses and scampered up to my bedroom, where I could catch my breath and slow my thudding heart.

My mind raced. She must have been out when I arrived, although there was still only my car. And she could have over-slept while I was up early this morning. I was going to have to share but I felt confident her thighs would make that bearable. I might even flirt a little, I told myself, feeling naughty.

Later, after several large glasses of wine, the words on the pages of the book I had picked up had started to blur and I raised my eyes to see Perry come into the room. I hadn't heard her come down the stairs and stared, momentarily mesmerised again by her sheer beauty.

She sat herself on the couch next to me and asked me to tell her about myself. So, I talked. And I talked, my tongue loosened by wine. I had forgotten what it was like for a woman to be interested in what I had to say. My ex had never listened and my voice had grown smaller and smaller, until it had existed only in a tiny corner of my mind. I heard words trip off my tongue to Perry, saw the smile crinkle the corner of her eyes when I made a joke, saw her brows knit together when I became sombre with my sentences. Before I knew it, my bottle was finished and it was time to go to bed. I had never been this relaxed in a female's company, especially one I was growing more and more attracted to.

As I got up reluctantly to head for bed, I asked her what she did.

"I collect butterflies," she said.

My days were spent sunning and swimming, and my evenings were spent chatting with Perry. Although I longed to kiss her more than anything in the world, it was the last thing I would do. Everywhere I went and looked, I was held back by the fear of rejection. It haunted me like a steady, silent terror.

I waited for Perry every evening with the anticipation reserved for a lover. I had felt this with my ex but that was a different time and I had been different then, too.

"What have you come to escape from?" Perry asked me. "We all come here to escape something."

I told her I had come to escape my heart-break.

"Legend has it," she told me, "that if you whisper a wish to a butterfly, then let it go, it will carry that wish and the Heavens will grant it."

Mostly though, she let me talk. She said little but what she said mattered. I opened myself to her, like a rose to the morning sun, and I soaked her in. Her eyes held mine when I spoke and I tingled in a secret place.

I began to dread that passage of time that I was helpless to stop. I wanted to slow the hours each evening, when I had Perry to myself, so that I could hold my beating heart in both hands and lay it in front of her. I have always given my love away like it's on special offer, like it's something that needs to be gotten rid of. For once I had a worthy recipient.

All my life, I had tried to be *"the one"* for someone else. I threw myself into a corner and called it compromise. I buried my happiness with a spade because it wasn't important, not compared with what my ex felt. I held my head up high because I was making her life complete and was giving her what she wanted. And she still cheated on me.

But, what did I feel? What did I *feel*?

I was so fixated on my heart being broken that I hadn't noticed it mend. A little love takes a little mending.

I thought of my ex. Gayle. Her name was Gayle. I could say it now without an ice-cold knife of torment tearing into me. I saw it in her eyes when the love was gone but I held on, fearing her rejection. Now that it has been and gone, I am no worse or better off. Her love washed over me as a tepid shower and I stand out now, naked and brave. I was intact and ready to begin all over again. You see, no matter how hard we try, we can't help but swap heart-break for love. Love is what wakes us in the morning: having it, the promise of it or the hope.

I felt the tickle of a million butterflies land on my sun-kissed arms, as Perry walked towards me. A million butterflies took flight, raising every hair on my arms, flying through every vein, running up every muscle. I felt the air from my nostrils as I panted, tickling my top lip, creating my smile.

In my head, I leant over the wall of a castle and I used both hands to heave out my pain. From the castle gates, I emerged as me.

With my eyes I saw Perry but with my heart I saw hope and that is what strangled my breath in my throat. The hope of her delicate fingers curled around my neck, as she pulled me closer for an embrace. The hope that one day I might wake up next to her and know that, in my heart, a million butterflies might land and pull me apart with love when they flew away.

Because love is a butterfly explosion. It's not meant to be a tepid shower, or a month where a bruised ego sulks. It's the all or nothing of the soul.

When it's nothing, it's easy to let go.

It was my last morning. Fear lay heavy on me because it was my final chance to tell Perry that I liked her. Words dissolved on my tongue before they could be spoken, disappearing like snowflakes in the sunshine.

I ran downstairs, hoping to find her staring out the kitchen window as she so often was but the room was empty. I made my way back up the stairs to check the other two bedrooms. They both stood empty, collecting dust.

I had missed her. Perry had gone.

I packed my bags and said goodbye to the house that had been my home for a month. Driving away, I wiped a salty tear from my cheek, kissed the wiping finger and took in my pain. Would I really never see Perry again? The woman who had taught me that I had a voice worth listening to and that the words I spoke mattered. Life takes you to people for a reason. When you swim forward through oceans of despair, there is always a butterfly collector.

I held keys in my hand as though they could open the kingdom of Heaven but, in fact, would open the door to that idyllic cottage I'd just spent a month in. I held them in my hands because I was scared to let go of them. That would be like letting go of Perry and I had so much more to say to her.

I was going to take my keys back, personally, and find out where Perry lived, or what her phone number was. You don't need much these days to make a connection. You don't get four weeks to know someone without a television or a mobile phone to interrupt the sentences that wrap around and tether you in the bonds of love. Love is won in the fall of an eyelid, not the spelling of a text.

I felt the same tension in my toes as I pulled my car up to where Mrs Milligan lived. The owner of the cottage where I had dreamt away my broken heart. I understood why a woman, who lived in an urban flat would hold ownership to where I had spent my summer, but I could not understand why she didn't live there. I would lose myself forever in those beach walks and winter winds.

"Hey, Mrs Milligan," I gushed, as she opened the door, inviting me in with trust, to take back her keys. "What a beautiful home you have."

"House," she corrected. "It's just a house."

"No," I went on, confident of my voice now, "It's a home: a house full of love. Thank you so much for renting to me."

"I'm glad you enjoyed. Is it all locked up?"

"Oh, yes. Here's my key. I don't know about Perry, she'd left before I could ask."

"Perry?" she said, her face white.

"Yes. Perry. The other woman who was staying there."

"Perry is my daughter," Mrs Milligan said. I smiled. Ah, free holiday cottage for the summer. That made sense.

"The butterfly collector?" I said.

Two fat teardrops raced down her cheeks. "That's her."

"I'm sorry," I said, perplexed. "Have I said something wrong?"

"Perry's dead," she smiled.

The ice-cold knife pierced me.

"No...no...," I stammered. "We spent every night together. We talked, we laughed, we..."

What *did* we do?

I talked every night to someone I assumed had already eaten, assumed had been busy all day while I swam and sunbathed, assumed didn't drink while I had swallowed the wine.

We had never touched. I had never lain my lips on hers, with my eyes closed, dreaming of a future together where I might make her smile. The electricity I had felt had come from my mind, seeing her mind.

I was in love with a ghost. I could cry.

Her mother said, "She died ten years ago but I can see for you it's today. For me, it's every day."

A flurry of words became strangled inside me. "What happened to her?" I finally managed.

"She took herself to the cottage, after the breakdown of her relationship. Her letter to me said she couldn't live with her broken heart and she killed herself. I can't live in that house but I can't sell it either. It was where she escaped."

"But...but she was beautiful," I stammered.

"Beautiful people can't see themselves," Mrs Milligan said. "She couldn't see hope."

I fluttered away...

I drove fast, away from Perry's mum, until I couldn't see. The rain that fell from the clouds and from my eyes blurred my windscreen, every teardrop falling from Heaven. I scrambled out of my car, slamming shut the door, as I staggered and slid my way into the park where I sometimes came to listen to my thoughts.

The rain fell on me in heavy drops, soaking my hair and clothes and, as I walked to a favourite bench where trees hung their branches in a motherly embrace, I began to smile.

Oh, Perry. Poor, poor wasted life. She had a heart that had taken mine and sewed it back together with her delicate love-stitching. I told myself to breathe and think of the words she had told me. She had given me a lesson.

She had taught me that love will heal a broken heart and no pain is ever the end, despite her learning the hardest way. I smiled to the clouds above, amidst my tears. Love is a lesson that goes hand-in-hand with life, and it sometimes hurts.

Perry took my heart to show me that beyond every heart-break is another love that can flourish. Nothing is ever the end, and from a seed a flower will grow.

A butterfly came then, vibrant orange and black, and bold with its bravery, as it found its legs and lowered itself onto my outstretched palm.

I remembered a story that Perry had told me about the Nagas of Assam, who believed that the dead go through transformations in the underworld until they are finally reborn as butterflies. When the butterfly dies, that is the end of the soul. There is no coming back.

I looked into the eyes of the beautiful butterfly, with tears and my heart ripping in two, its dark eyes whispering to the corners of me and I held it to my lips, whispering a wish.

It flew away then but it left me with hope.

KAREN CAMPBELL is the author of *The Knowing*, *Violet's Story* and a collection of short stories called *Little Whispers*, all available as e-books or paperbacks.

The Knowing is the first in a trilogy featuring Glasgow psychic Jen Keith and her police officer girlfriend, Kate Coutts. She is currently working on the second instalment, *A Love Like Ishinnie*.

She is working on another book called *The Dairy of a Fat Cow*, about the life of an over-weight Tesco night shift employee called Viv.

She has a million ideas and never enough seconds in the day.

www.facebook.com/Ringe70

twitter.com/RingeAlba

www.amazon.co.uk/Karen-Campbell/e/B00ITVNH5C/ref=ntt_dp_epwbk_0

IN BED WITH MISS LUCAS
Frances Gapper

CHARLOTTE WAS IN the apple garth, removing a comb from one of the beehives, when she noticed something moving in a shady place beneath the trees. A shape separated, becoming two, then merged again. A thing composed of humanity, of partly naked flesh. It was Mr Collins and her brother William.

Her arms were sleeved in crawling bees – she wore no protection, only a muslin smock over her dress – and intent not to disturb them more than the task required, she remained still. Honey dripped from the comb.

Mr Collins shouted out, then uttered a blasphemy, while slapping at his nether parts. A bee had stung him. They are intelligent, even witty creatures; this one died for its joke.

"Don't tell, Charlotte, because I never tell on you." She did not at once understand William's passing remark, made under his breath. When the meaning of his words became clear to her, she was outraged by the sordid comparison.

"It is an entirely different thing!" she muttered to herself in the laundry room, while attending to her brother's seducer. A blue bag had been found effective to draw the sting and soothe the hurt. Now Mr Collins was lecturing her upon her good fortune; upon the affability and condescension of Lady Catherine de Bourgh. Would the man never be quiet?

She returned the bottle of saltpetre to the shelf; he proposed to her. It was not romantic. This was Lady Catherine's own suggestion, apparently, made upon receiving the news of Miss Elizabeth Bennet's refusal of her protégé. He proudly displayed Lady Catherine's letter, of which she could make out very little, since – as was her Ladyship's habit – it was narrowly crossed and untidily written. However, she was not insensible to the many advantages of such an arrangement: principally, the freedom it would give her. She took a moment to consider, then accepted his proposal – or rather, his patron's decision.

Lady Catherine had already written several letters to Charlotte, containing detailed instructions on such matters as the keeping of poultry and self-education. Miss Lucas had not perused these with any great attention: better to preserve the flattering idea of this great lady's favour than to consider seriously whether the relationship would be likely to promote long-lasting happiness and content.

As for Mr Collins: well. Her parents would be delighted, since he would succeed to the possession of Longbourn after Mr Bennet's death, and the match would thereby allow them to triumph over their neighbours. The younger girls might now form hopes of *coming out* a year or two sooner than they might otherwise have done; and the boys would be relieved from their apprehension of Charlotte's dying an old maid. The least agreeable circumstance in the business was the surprise it must occasion to Elizabeth Bennet, whose friendship she valued beyond that of any other person, by whose opinions she was most often guided, and whose trust she had betrayed.

Elizabeth set down the candle. She said, "Lydia will keep poor Jane up half the night, I daresay, with her usual nonsensical chatter of officers and gentlemen."

"It was good of Jane, to allow me to usurp her place in your bed."

"Jane is always good," Elizabeth sighed. "Too good, I sometimes think."

Charlotte unlaced her friend's corset, kissed the back of her neck and left her standing in her chemise. "I must speak to you, Eliza, of a matter which perhaps will shock you." She then disclosed the matter of her own recent correspondence with Lady Catherine.

Elizabeth had often felt that Miss Lucas's nature was very different from her own; but that she could encourage such a person, seemed almost as far from possibility as that Elizabeth could encourage Lady Catherine herself, and her astonishment was consequently so great as to overcome at first the bounds of decorum, and she could not help crying out, "Lady Catherine de Bourgh! My dear Charlotte – impossible!"

Miss Lucas seemed a little perturbed on receiving so direct a reproach; though, as it was no more than she expected, she soon regained her composure and crossed an ankle over her knee before replying, "Why should you be surprised, my dear Eliza? Do you consider yourself to be the only person with a claim to my attentions? Or do you think it incredible that Lady Catherine should be able to procure any woman's good opinion, because she has not been so happy as to secure yours?"

But Elizabeth had now recollected herself, and making a strong effort, was able to assure Miss Lucas with tolerable firmness that the prospect of their intimacy was highly grateful to her, and that she wished her all imaginable happiness.

"Thank you."

"Be so good as to tell me, Charlotte, how the two of you became acquainted?"

"Lady Catherine heard of me by reputation," Charlotte replied delicately. "We have exchanged portraits. You may recall that Maria sketched me in the character of Rosalind? She prefers that one above the rest."

"She will make you cut off your hair." Elizabeth got into bed and punched one of the pillows.

"I should not mind it." Miss Lucas joined her friend.

"You must know that she is a relation of Mr Darcy."

"Yes, and I intend you to marry him, so that we may continue to meet often."

"I am afraid, then, Charlotte, you will be sadly disappointed."

The conversation broke off and did not resume for a while, partly because Miss Lucas had her hand over Elizabeth's mouth, to stop her from screaming out loud. At length she said, "Well?"

Attempting to control her breath, Elizabeth said, "I will think on the matter, Charlotte."

"Good. I have not yet talked to you of Mr Collins."

"Pray do not talk of him at all."

"I must, and then we will leave the subject entirely."

Jane confessed herself a little surprised at the prospect of a liaison between Miss Lucas and Lady Catherine, but she said less of her astonishment than of her earnest desire for their happiness. Nor could Elizabeth persuade her to consider it as unlikely.

"My dear Jane! Your sweetness and disinterestedness are really angelic. But in truth, it is impossible for any one woman to retain Miss Lucas's undivided affections. She is not romantic."

"Oh, my poor Lizzie."

"I am now tempted to make another acquaintance myself. What think you of Miss Bingley?"

"Well..." Jane hesitated.

"Of course I am joking."

Lady Catherine had expressed an inclination to see Pemberley again, and was determined that Charlotte should accompany her.

"The family is not down for the summer, or certainly I should not think of it. Miss Elizabeth Bennet, as she was before she ensnared my nephew into this disgraceful marriage, must not expect to be noticed by his family and friends, having willfully acted against the inclinations of all. Nay, she must be censured, slighted and despised by everyone connected with him."

Charlotte said nothing in return – her mind was too full for conversation, her spirits too low – and both remained silent as they entered the park. A stream of some natural importance was swelled into greater, but without any artificial appearance. Its banks were neither formal, nor falsely adorned. How unlike Rosings Park, Lady Catherine's residence!

As their carriage drew near to the house, Charlotte was overcome by apprehension lest they should have been misinformed. She longed to see Elizabeth again, yet dreaded the thought of meeting her in company with Mr Darcy, or in Lady

Catherine's presence. That Mr Darcy was equally anxious to prevent such a gathering, she felt sure.

Once admitted into the hall, they were greeted by the housekeeper. As they passed into other rooms, Charlotte observed less splendour, but more real elegance, than she was accustomed to see at Rosings. Her own home on Lady Catherine's estate was rather small, but well built and convenient, and when Mr Collins could be forgotten – as he often was – it provided great comfort.

Lady Catherine lamented some changes made to the disposition of the furniture in her nephew's house and deplored the old-fashioned curtains, while attributing all perceived lapses in taste to Elizabeth. "She has improved the place so little and wrought such harm!" Unable to listen further, Charlotte excused herself and hurried from the room. She saw the housekeeper's surprise, and Lady Catherine looked very displeased. Quickly she left the house and walked away, hardly knowing which direction she took.

A circuit walk led to a path that descended among hanging woods. She crossed the river by a simple bridge and followed a narrow walk. Upon entering a clearing, to her great surprise, there before her she saw Elizabeth and another woman. They were within ten yards of her, and so abrupt was her arrival that it was impossible to avoid an encounter. Charlotte's eyes met Elizabeth's, and the cheeks of each were overspread with the deepest blush. For a moment, both seemed immoveable from surprise, but shortly recovering themselves, they advanced and spoke, if not in terms of perfect composure, at least of perfect civility.

Mrs Darcy was very obviously expecting a child, but said nothing of her condition. She introduced Charlotte to her companion, Mr Darcy's sister Georgiana. The young woman was also blushing, though for no apparent reason. Her manners were unassuming and gentle, and she seemed exceedingly shy. She curtseyed and held out her hand; Charlotte, without thinking, took and kissed it. This made Georgiana gasp, and Elizabeth smile.

In the years that immediately followed, Charlotte received several letters from Elizabeth, giving information about her growing family; and these never failed to mention Georgiana. "My sister asks to be remembered to you – commands me to say that – would be glad to have news of you." Charlotte kept the letters in her desk. She perceived that Mrs Darcy was hard put to dampen the enthusiastic admiration of her young relative for a person she had met just once in a glade.

Charlotte herself had thought Miss Darcy pleasant enough, with sense and good humour in her face: but she wished only for the friend of her own youth. Too well persuaded of the value of all she had lost, or willfully thrown away, she mourned her own perverseness of feeling, while knowing how improbable it was that they should ever again be united on terms of mutual cordiality.

Their correspondence ceased for a while; until at last Mrs Darcy wrote again. This time, there was no message from Georgiana. She had moved, with a friend, to Llangollen in Wales, and was living there in sweet retirement – according to Elizabeth, "in neatness, elegance and taste".

Upon the sudden death of Mr Collins – from a cold he caught while reciting the burial service, together with many encomiums, at Lady Catherine's graveside in a sharp easterly wind – Mr Darcy travelled to Rosings from Derbyshire. He brought his private chaplain to chant Mr Collins's own requiem, and his wife to console the grieving widow as best she might.

The years had wrought their changes and Mr Darcy, now florid and portly, went off to the funeral in the highest good humour, without betraying any apprehension as to the wisdom or the propriety of leaving Elizabeth alone with Mrs Collins. Alone they effectively were in the drawing room of Rosings, for Lady Catherine's daughter Anne, grown from a peevish and sickly young woman to an autocratic matron, was employing her time usefully in itemising the linen cupboard.

After a little silence, Charlotte said, "You are as beautiful as ever, Eliza."

"My dear, you flatter me. When a woman has three grown-up daughters, she ought to give over thinking of her own beauty."

"I don't believe you ever thought of it much."

Elizabeth picked at the chair's arm. "Lady Catherine's death must have dealt you a great blow."

"It was a surprise. One evening we quarrelled over a trifle, as was not unusual. I went up to bed, taking leave of her with very little courtesy, and she died of a stroke, in that chair." Elizabeth stood up quickly. "We found her in the morning, still seated upright, as though turned to stone."

"How horrible!"

"Let us talk of more cheerful matters. Have you heard lately from Miss Darcy?"

"Yes, I thank you. She is well, and I believe most happy. What a charming view from this window! And what will you do now, Charlotte? How will you live?"

"Both my husband and Lady Catherine have left me well provided for. Perhaps I shall take lodgings in Bath."

"Will you live alone?"

"I think so. Unless you will come with me."

Elizabeth did not turn around. "There was a time – we could perhaps – but it is too late now."

"I did not know such a thing was possible."

"Sometimes one must force a way to others' acceptance. I never loved my husband so well as when he gave way at last to Georgiana's pleas. Otherwise I think she must have died of grief, for she would not part with her friend. Ah – it is a pity, a pity." Elizabeth walked up the room and down again. "I wish that custom did not forbid us to attend Mr Collins's funeral, for at least then we might get some fresh air. To be confined indoors – unbearable!"

"Shall we go upstairs? It is lighter there."

"Oh! Very well."

As they ascended the grand staircase, Charlotte said, "I could not love her."

"Of course not. It was never in your nature to suffer another's will to override your own. But the question remains, Charlotte, whether you are capable of giving your heart to anyone."

"Did you give yours – I mean, to your husband?"

138

"Yes. We were very much in love. I did not marry him at your bidding."

"I never believed so."

"And yet; and yet. This is hard to say. Well. My thoughts oftentimes flew away to you. I remembered how after we had – been together, in bed – you would wait, and after a little while, you would ask, 'Are you ready for me again?' And that helped; if you take my meaning. It raised up my nature."

They crossed the upper landing and entered a large, airy bedchamber. Charlotte locked the door behind them. She said, "You need not be afraid. Catherine never came in here."

"What is that to me?" Elizabeth held out her hand for the key.

Charlotte gave it to her. "And you likewise would never suffer another's will to override yours."

Elizabeth held the key against her lips for a few moments, considering; then she walked to the window and placed it on the sill. She threw open the casement. At once the fresh and sweet smell of lilac rushed into the room, with the singing of many birds.

"Are you ready for me again?" Charlotte asked her.

###

FRANCES GAPPER's story collection, *Absent Kisses,* was published by Diva Books in 2002 and a flash fiction booklet, *The Tiny Key,* by Sylph Editions in 2009. One of my stories was included in *Let's Call the Whole Thing Off*, a Penguin anthology of arguments, edited by Ali Smith, Sarah Wood and Kasia Boddy; others have appeared in the *London Magazine* online, the *Reader's Digest*, Ireland-based magazine *The Moth* and Plymouth University's *Short Fiction*.

LOVE MATCH
Jade Winters

MOTHERS AND THEIR toddlers sat on the floor in the corner of Joanne's local library. Every Monday morning without fail they would be there singing *Five Little Ducks* in an out of tune babble. Tuesday evening it was the romance book club, where women would meet to either totally obliterate a book they'd read or gush over its handsome heroes. Wednesday was "Knit and natter", Thursday "Baby wriggle and rhyme" and Friday "Computers for the over 50s". The fact that Joanne knew the timetable of the library by heart was quite worrying.

She peeked above her book and watched as a librarian with wavy hair pushed a trolley along the aisle. Joanne couldn't tear her eyes away from the woman's temptingly curved mouth as she slowly ran her tongue over her lips when she stopped to insert a book on the shelf. Joanne gripped the edges of the book she held between her hands. She really was going to have to get over this – she was acting like a stalker. No doubt the poor woman had a trail of kids and a hunky husband to snuggle up with on a cold winter's night.

If she really believed this, why did she find herself coming to the library at every given opportunity, just to be in the same space as the woman who had stolen her heart from the moment she'd laid eyes on her? Oh, she'd given off the persona of being a respectable librarian, but Joanne had caught sight of the lotus flower tattoo on her shoulder when her cardigan had slipped. She wasn't as prim and proper as her exterior suggested. And what an exterior it was. Not only did her face possess a natural beauty, she had also been blessed with a body that was tall and graceful.

What Joanne wanted more than anything was to put a name to the face. She silently cursed the jobsworth who had decided to do away with staff members having to wear name tags.

Her stomach rumbled loudly. *Time to go home*. Reluctantly she pushed her chair back and rose to her feet. The librarian looked across at her and their eyes met momentarily before Joanne glanced away. It was like an unspoken ritual between them – each time Joanne was about to leave they somehow always seemed to lock eyes. Maybe she was reading too much into it. The woman was most probably making sure Joanne wasn't going to do anything crazy. *I really do have to get a life*. She pulled her jacket hood over her head and walked out into the pouring rain.

Twenty minutes later she stepped through the door of her ground floor flat and into the yellow painted hallway. She shrugged off her wet jacket and hung it up on a hook, before bending down and scooping up the pile of envelopes scattered across the floor. She shuffled through them as she walked to the kitchen. *Bills, bills, more bills, ah what's this*? A letter with a blazing gold stamp read; *You're a winner*. She frowned and scratched her head. Had someone made a mistake? As she tore at the envelope she racked her brain trying to remember if she'd entered any competitions. The only thing that came to mind was a questionnaire she'd filled out about her ideal partner. She had only completed it for the chance to win an iPad, but in all honesty she hadn't expected anything to come of it.

A weekend in Paris with the partner of your dreams – the title promised in large black font. She groaned, convinced it was a scam; further down the page she'd be asked for bank details or a cheque to cover admin fees. She quickly read on. Nope, no financial extortion techniques, just text informing her that she'd won a night at the Ritz Paris, at which dinner would be served for her and her mystery love match. It finished by giving various dates which started as early as the following week.

Sounded simple enough but she wasn't that desperate that she'd go on a blind date with a stranger in Paris; not yet anyway. Yes, she was aware that Love Match's computer system had a stellar reputation of achieving a 99.9% success rate for matching people with their ideal mate, but not even that was enough to persuade her.

No iPad, no can do! She tossed the letter onto the worktop and took out a loaf of bread from the cupboard.

Feeling her mobile phone vibrate in her back pocket, she withdrew it and glanced down at the screen.

"Hey Mum. How's it going?" She held the phone away from her ear waiting for the oncoming barrage of complaints.

Joanne spoke at all the appropriate moments. She ummed and ahhed when her mum told her about the neighbour with gout, the affair her boss was having with the cleaning lady, and finally about the man across the road she'd seen pleasuring himself through his bedroom window.

Joanne pulled a face. "Ah Mum that's gross. I'm just about to make lunch," she said, trying to erase the image of her mum's very hairy neighbour – naked.

"Well what about poor me? How did you think I felt? I told your dad this neighbourhood was going downhill. He wouldn't listen," she complained.

Joanne rolled her eyes. She desperately wanted to tell her that this could all have been avoided if she'd just stop spying on the neighbours through her net curtains, but didn't think that would go down too well. Instead she remained silent.

"Anyway, I only called to tell you your dad and I are coming to stay with you next weekend."

Dread filled Joanne. "Um next weekend?" How was she going to get out of this one? She couldn't lie. Her mother's ear served as a highly functioning lie detector – she would have been an ideal asset to an insurance company.

"Yes, is that a problem?"

She could imagine her mum's foot tapping away impatiently. "Um yes it's just that..." She glanced towards the letter. There was only one thing for it. "It's just that I won't be here. I'm going away."

"Where you going?" her mum asked, suspicion in her voice.

Oh shit. What could be worse than having to spend the whole weekend with her parents? "I'm going to Paris," she said with a brightness she didn't feel.

"To where?" her mum barked.

"Paris, Mum."

"What you going there for?" she asked accusingly.

"I won it in a competition."

"Have you lost your mind?"

Joanne smiled, looking down at the letter again. Not her mind but maybe just maybe she'd lose her heart. *Paris, here I come.*

The Ritz Paris was every bit as glamorous as she'd imagined.

"Dinner will be served at seven thirty," the French man said as he slowly backed out of the room and closed the door gently.

She only had a vague recollection of how she had filled out the questionnaire. If it had been on one of her *I won't ever find anyone to love* days, maybe it was best that she couldn't recall the details. Her mind was full of wonder as she slipped into a pair of black trousers followed by a sequined silver vest top. One last brush of her thick sandy hair and she was ready. In an hour she'd either still be downstairs enjoying herself or back in her room wishing she had not wasted her time.

"Bonjour, Mademoiselle," the maître d' said with a small smile. Though she wasn't one for stereotyping she couldn't help but notice the striking resemblance to Inspector Poirot – with his upward curled moustache and chubby face.

"Bonjour, Monsieur. J'ai réservations pour le dîner à sept heures et demie." Her school French teacher would have been proud.

His smile broadened. "Oui, your guest has also arrived."

Joanne gulped. "She has?"

"Oui, Mademoiselle, follow me please," he said with a click of the heels.

Joanne trailed behind him as he confidently weaved his way around the tables as if he were wearing skates, before stopping at one where a lone woman sat. From the back it looked like Joanne was onto a winner – Love Match had got her hair colour correct. A brunette. Taking a deep breath she readied herself as she reached the table and looked down at the woman. Her head began to spin at such a speed she thought she might faint. The woman stood and held her by the elbow — instead of helping, it only made things worse.

"It's ok," the woman said to maître d'. "Could you bring some water please?"

With a puzzled look on his face, he nodded. "Oui."

"Here, take a seat," the woman said, easing Joanne into the chair opposite.

Joanne combed her fingers through her hair. "I'm...sor...sorry. I just don't understand."

"I have to admit this is quite a shock for me as well," the woman said, leaning towards her. "But a very pleasant one," she added with a smile.

Joanne shook her head in confusion. "But...ho...how?"

The woman shrugged. "I guess we'll have to wait and see if Love Match really knows its stuff, but from initial impressions I think it's spot on."

Joanne stared at the woman, her eyes widening. "Your name? What's your name?" she asked, her voice getting a little stronger.

"Elizabeth, but my friends call me Lizzie."

Joanne leaned back in her chair. *Lizzie.* She finally knew the name of the librarian who had stolen her heart.

###

JADE WINTERS While Jade has been putting words together since she was a child, it wasn't until 2010 that she became a serious writer.

Today, as a full-time author, she has published several novels in the lesbian fiction genre as well as a number of short stories.

Jade was born and educated in London where she studied journalism for three years at a London University. She now makes her home in Dorset in the South of England with her partner and their furry companions - Buttons, Zorro and Zeus.

www.jade-winters.com

FRANKIE AND OTHER F-WORDS
Tanith Nyx

FATAL, FODDER, Flotsam. Today was filled with F-words. Not fun, fabulous or fantastic F-words, but frank, forthright, fornicating F-words.

Sam took a long draw on her cigarette and exhaled a chain of smoke rings into the air. She checked her Blackberry or rather pretended to check her Blackberry. In truth she just wanted to look at that text, the one from Sheena sent at 3:46 am, the one typed in so much drunken text speak it looked like cuneiform. None-the-less Sam understood it perfectly.

She chipped her cigarette out in the ashtray next to the bed and threw back the duvet. She could still taste Tequila. Using the walls as a guide, she careened down the hall to the bathroom where she dropped to her knees and wrapped her arms around the cold toilet bowl.

Today was filled with F-words: Frankie. Fuck- fucked- fucking Frankie...

Sam wished she was still drunk and could stay that way forever. Forever wasn't one of today's F-words. Time was running out for Sam. And for Sheena.

It had already run out for Frankie.

Sam grabbed the towel rail and tried to hoist herself back to standing but another aftershock hit. She retched until her stomach was empty then rolled over on the bathmat and curled up into a ball, hugging her knees tight to her chest.

She could hear her mobile ringing. Every time it went to answerphone there was a brief pause before it began ringing again. Sam gathered all her strength and staggered like a drugged wild animal back to her bedroom. She stumbled and hit her head on the corner edge of the bedside table. Just what the hell had she taken

145

last night? She held the phone to her ear; a bloody gash had opened and blood was dripping down the side of her face.

"Sam, what are we going to do?" Sheena's voice blasted panic down the phone.

"Do what you want. We're dead now anyway."

"Sam, this is fucking serious. They don't have the death penalty in this country."

"Then we're worse than dead."

"But it was an accident."

Sam wandered into the kitchen holding her head. When she pulled her hand away blood seeped between her fingers. She tore some kitchen paper from the roll and held it to her head. "Do you think the cops are going to believe it was an accident?"

"Not really. But what can we do?"

Sam had hoped with every ounce of her being that it had all been some drugged-up hallucination – that she'd imagined the whole thing. But Sheena's text and her calling confirmed that it had really happened.

"Sam, are you still there?"

Sam dropped the phone onto the counter top and began to hunt for the paracetamol. Her blood dripped into the drawer as she fumbled through pens, loose batteries and corkscrews looking for a blister pack. She slammed the drawer closed, dropped to her knees and began to cry uncontrollably – for Frankie at first but then for herself. At least Frankie was free.

Sam turned her gaze to the flyer on the fridge, the flyer for the Clit Club, first Friday of every month. Sam snatched it down, tearing it into tiny pieces. "Why? Why did I have to go this month?" She cried. She had considered staying in and watching Netflix but Sheena had been so persuasive. That's how fuck buddies are. And Sam had a rubber arm, easy to twist. It was only supposed to be a bit of no-strings fun.

Sam stood up and lit another cigarette. Her hands were trembling. She began to pace. Frankie. Frankie the femme from Finsbury Park. So many F-words in such a short space. They should have turned her down. Should have left the chem- sex to the boys.

146

But when Frankie came over and asked if they were up for some fun what were they supposed to say? Frankie was fit and flirtatious and open to anything – *everything*. When she rolled up a twenty and pushed it into Sam's fist, Sam didn't think twice, she just snorted the line and handed the note over to Sheena.

"Sheena, meet Tina." Frankie had tittered, referring to the crystal meth. "You ladies are in for a treat." She winked. "This ice is smooth as silk – nothing like that chunky glass crap I had earlier." She licked the tip of her index finger and dabbed up the rest of the powder from her make-up mirror. "Now that we've all met, let's go back to yours and have us some real fun. Do you live far?"

Sheena had downed the rest of her pint, shaken her head and thrown Sam a look like they'd both won on the scratch cards. That was the moment they both should have run.

Sam stopped in front of the mirror and, seeing her reflection, impulsively punched the glass so hard it shattered. Her knuckles began to bleed.

A knock – no, a pounding – on the door broke the silence that followed.

Sam wondered how long she had been standing there, staring into the shards of glass at her feet. Fragmented.

"Where did you go?" Sheena shouted. "I was talking to you and suddenly you were gone. You scared the shit out of me."

Sam pulled Sheena into the doorway. "Can you shut up? Do you want to get us both arrested?"

Sheena stuffed her hands into her jeans pockets and stormed into the house. Sam quickly closed the door behind her.

"It's ok for you," Sheena said. "You don't have a naked corpse handcuffed in your shower."

Sam looked down at her plain white tee, speckled with the blood from her head. Apart from a pair of black knickers it was the only thing she had on. She pumped her knuckles, watching the beads of blood rise and break through the skin. "I used to fucking love Fridays." She spoke softly from some faraway place inside herself.

"Snap out of it, will you?" Sheena slammed her fist down on the kitchen table, punctuating. "Get your shit together; we have to get out of here."

"And go where exactly?" Sam rejoined the conversation, fuming with the futility of the suggestion. "I haven't got a penny left after last night. I'm four days from payday. Like what the fuck, Sheen... Are we gonna run for it on foot? —coz I don't think I have enough on my Oyster card to even get the fucking bus."

"Don't worry about that, I have money." Sheena opened the fridge door, "Got any beer? I need a hair of the dog."

"You are joking." Sam threw her hands up and swaggered back to the bedroom. She allowed herself to fall, face-first, sideways across the bed. A new wave of F-words were foisting themselves upon her. Finished. Futureless. Finito.

Sheena had found a bottle of Desperado behind the chicken curry meal-for-one and was chugging it down as she came into the bedroom. She sat on the edge of the bed, belched and let the empty bottle slip from her fingers to the floor. "You were the one that killed her." She leant forward, resting her elbows on her knees.

Sam rolled over, a look of ferocity on her face. "Excuse me?? —it was you that suggested edgeplay."

"No, it was Frankie." Sheena rubbed her flat hand over her hair. "She wanted us to tie her up and—"

"So?" Sam bounded off the bed, reaching for her cigarettes. "That's not what killed her. You had to go one step further, break out the blindfold and cuffs and—"

"And everything would have been fine if you hadn't covered her nose and mouth for so long..."

A long silence passed between them before Sam spoke again. "She was enjoying it – she didn't even try to give the stop signal – and you know it... You were there... it doesn't make any sense."

"We are so fucking dead." Sheena cradled her head between her elbows, rocking herself gently.

"I can't go to prison; freedom means everything to me." Sam sucked her cigarette so hard it crushed the filter. "I would rather die than go down for this."

Sheena lifted her head, her eyebrows arched high and her eyes widened in a *Eureka!* expression.

Sam knew that look. It was the same look Sheena had on her face that first night they met at Substation in Soho. Sheena had been leaning against the corrugated fence in her red tag 501s and her oversized vest (that you could see right into when she didn't have her arms crossed) when Sam strolled over and asked if she wanted to shoot a game of pool. Two hours and ten games later, Sheena got that look. Next thing Sam knew they were both outside in the alley on the bonnet of a parked car. Sam's leather trousers were down around her knees, her bare buttocks flat against the cold pressed steel, Sheena passionately kissing her stomach with her fist pumping deep up inside of her.

The alley had started to spin as Sheena buried her face between Sam's slippery thighs. They'd attracted a sizeable audience by the time Sam had dug her fingernails into Sheena's shoulders while arching her back and announcing for all to hear that she was coming! So too was the club's bouncer – red-faced with rage – looking like Boudica on the rampage.

Sam had scrambled down off the car pulling her trousers up as she ran, laughing wildly, arm-in-arm with Sheena, followed by the fading, spontaneous applause of faceless strangers. And a barrage of abusive threats from the incensed bouncer, including the unmistakeable phrase 'barred for life'.

When Sam and Sheena then realised they only lived three streets away from one another, they knew it must be fate. They had tried dating after that but it only lasted three weeks. They had bonded in the height of an adrenaline-fuelled orgasm and the 'honey-I'm-home-let's-go-to-IKEA' routine couldn't compete.

Instead they became each other's bad influence: Dial-a-buddy-besties with full-on fetish benefits. In the six years since they'd met, Sam had come to know that when Sheena had that look on her face, trouble wasn't far behind.

"We'll go out in a blaze of glory." Sheena's Eureka face softened as her pupils widened.

"No way..." Sam chipped her cigarette into the ashtray and wrapped her quivering arms around Sheena's shoulders, squeezing her hard. She kissed the top of her head. "It was just supposed to be a bit of fun – none of this was supposed to happen."

"Would you rather run the gauntlet of razors, or fall in a field of flowers? You said it yourself, freedom is everything. You don't want to get banged up for life. I don't want to get banged up for life. This way it's still us in control. We'll be famous – like Bonnie & Clyde or Sid & Nancy."

"No, we'll be like Bonnie & Bonnie or Nancy & Nancy, dumbass." Sam massaged Sheena's shoulders deep with the thumbs of both hands. She smiled darkly, her mind folding in on itself like a cascading house of cards.

"OK, Thelma & Louise then." Sheena pulled free from Sam's embrace and planted a large wet kiss on Sam's mouth.

"...Kiss of death." Sam whispered, still drunk on the taste of Sheena's desire, still wasted from last night's cocktail of class As. Sheena was right; Sam didn't want to get banged up for life. Truth be told, even a day would be too long. She would be like one of those emaciated tigers at the zoo, pacing back and forth in front of the bars, flies buzzing around her head, psychologically traumatised by her infernal captivity. Factor in the guilt and regret that was already beginning to fester... *What if she really had covered Frankie's face for too long?* "OK, but—"

"But what?" Sheena took Sam's hands into her own and looked her straight in the eye.

"I don't want it to hurt."

"Leave it to me babe." Sheena stuffed her fists deep into her pockets and vanished out the door.

In a moment of insane complicity the deal had been sealed.

When Sheena returned, Sam was soaking in a hot, soapy bath.

Sheena locked the front door and began to undress, dropping her clothes in a trail on the way to the bathroom. She stepped into the bath; the rhinestone on her navel piercing sparkled in the light. She looked down at Sam and raised her eyebrows playfully. "Watersports?"

"Not even funny." Sam tried to smile as a last, lost courtesy of their fated friendship, but her lip merely trembled and a lone tear rolled down her cheek.

Sheena shrugged and lowered herself into the tub across from Sam; then she opened her closed fists. Across one palm, two loaded skinny syringes, across the other a yellowed rubber tourniquet.

Sam looked longingly at Sheena – her forever friend, her fuck buddy, her partner in crime – and she kissed her, deeply – desperately – for the very last time. She pulled away, weak, drained. "We had some fun though, didn't we?"

"We did." Sheena smiled with one half of her mouth, trying hard not to cry.

Sam held out her upturned arm and allowed Sheena to tie her off, a last act of intimacy between them. She bit her lip as the needle pierced her skin. A cold sensation washed over her from her head to her toes.

"I love you, Sam," Sheena said as she tapped three fingers briskly against her own arm. She flicked the back of her fingernail against the syringe and slid the needle into the raised vein.

Sam watched Sheena through droopy eyelids as Sheena slumped down in the water, flat and floppy, like a euthanized puppy. Sam wanted to stroke Sheena's hair, but she couldn't lift her arm.

As the heroin numbed Sam's veins, her life slowly draining away, she heard a strong familiar voice. She recognised him from the club. What did he want? He was banging so hard on the door, calling in through the letterbox like the place was on fire.

"Sam! It's me, Paul. Are you in there?" Bang-bang-bang on the door. "Sam, don't touch the meth – there's a bad batch going around – five people from the club are dead. Sam, are you in there? For fuck sake, Sam – open the fucking door!"

Sam sighed a final breath of bitter relief. They hadn't killed Frankie after all. She closed her eyes and faded into fatal darkness.

F's everywhere.

###

TANITH NYX is an author under construction. In previous incarnations she has published poetry, erotica, flash fiction and a sci-fi novel for children. She is currently working on a psychedelic time-travelling LesFic novel, which she hopes to be finished by 1981 – or in the near future. Her work has been described as Unique, Dark, Quirky, Funny, and Please just let me go... I'll say whatever you want me to say; please, I have a family. She lives in a leafy London suburb with her wife, teenage son and a rescued Staffordshire bull terrier named Pixie. www.tanithnyx.com

JUST THE WAY YOU ARE
Andrea Bramhall

"I HAVE AN appointment." My voice shakes when I say that. Maybe it's because I'm going to let someone, the lovely Emma, who I don't know all that well, cut this shaggy mop I call hair. But more likely it's because I don't know her nearly as well as I want to.

The girl pops a bubble of chewing gum and looks down at the diary. "Name?"

"Dani."

"Right." She manages to draw the word out and make it last for about two seconds before she starts blowing another bubble.

I want to stick my finger in it and make it burst on her face. I can just picture that sticky pink goo stuck on the end of her nose when I do. Serves her right for being rude. Of course, I don't. But that doesn't stop me smiling at the thought of it.

"Emma's still with her last client right now," she says, and points to a small sofa with its back to the window. "You can sit there till she's done." Bubblegum girl dismisses me and goes back to the time consuming, brain taxing task of blowing bigger bubbles while staring out of the window and twirling hair around one's finger. Multitasking at its finest.

I shake my head. I shouldn't bitch and I shouldn't make assumptions. I hate when people do that to me, and I don't want to be a hypocrite. We all have to start somewhere and at least she's working and not lying in bed like my younger sister – Lisa's three years younger than me and probably the same age as bubblegum girl. So I really shouldn't bitch, even if it is only thought bitchin', but I can't help it. It's what I do when I'm nervous. And right now, I'm really fucking nervous.

Feeling somewhat more charitable towards her I try to smile gratefully as I say thank you and sit down on the really, really uncomfortable sofa. Damn, that'd kill you if you had piles or some shit. I pick up a magazine to distract me from my aching backside and entertain myself until the lovely Emma is ready for me.

The salon is a large room with huge windows all along the front and a dividing wall up the middle to create another couple of stations for the stylists. It's Monday today. Slow day. So there's only Emma and the junior, A.K.A. bubblegum girl, working. I always try to come on a Monday if I can. Emma's friendlier when the older women aren't around.

I sneak a glance over to where she's working. Standing with her back to me as she moves around the old lady getting her blue rinse, chatting as she works diligently to blow dry every strand. Her own strawberry blonde hair's twisted into an elegant...erm, twist...at the back of her head. I'm sure that has some fancy hairstylist name, but to me it just looks gorgeous and highlights her neck. That long neck that I want to taste. Her arse wiggles as she steps from one foot to the other. Now, when I say "wiggles" I mean it flexes. It undulates. It ripples. It...

"She's nearly done. If you follow me to the sink I'll wash your hair for you," bubblegum girl said before walking away to the sinks.

I shake myself out of one daydream and straight into another about the gum falling out of her mouth and dropping in my hair while she washes it. I don't think bald would be a good look for me. I have this dint in the top of my head from falling out of a treehouse when I was a kid. I'd just end up looking weird and shit. I just know it. But I can't say that without being rude. I mean what do you say...excuse me, Miss. Bubblegum, but can you remove the offensive gloop in your gob so that you don't accidentally spit it into my hair and make me look like a weirdo? Cheers, thanks. See? Not gonna happen.

"It's all right, Brittney. I've got it," Emma calls over her shoulder as she turns off her hairdryer and stows it quickly at her station. "If you can do a quick clean down for me I'll wash Dani's hair." She smiles at me while she does something else with her hands. Takes off the woman's gown or something. I don't care. She's smiling at me. At me. Did you get that? At me. I think I'm smiling back. I must be. I catch a glimpse of myself in the mirror. Oh God. That looks more like a grimace than a smile. Shit. She's turned away.

She rolls up her sleeves as she walks to the sink. Is it my imagination or are her hips, those gorgeous curvy hips, rolling just a little bit more than normal?

"Dani?" She's smiling again as she stands by the sink, one hand on her hip, the other on the back of the chair, and one eyebrow arched mischievously. "Are you ready?"

I nod my head and hope I don't trip over my feet.

"Do you want me to take your coat, darlin', or would you rather keep it on?" She taps the sleeve of my jacket and manages to catch it as I shrug it from my shoulders and mumble my thanks.

She manoeuvres me easily into the chair, wraps a towel about my shoulders and presses me gently backward until I'm exactly where she wants me. And yes, I'm exactly where I want to be too. Looking straight into those baby blues and wondering if I'd ever have the courage to ask her the question on the tip of my tongue. *Can I take you for a drink?*

Her fingers are soft against my neck as she sweeps hair from under my collar and pulls the cloth down as far as she can so it won't get wet. If I didn't know any better, I'd have sworn her eyes dropped down my neck and focussed on the dip between my collar bones. But I'm sure I do know better, and someone as beautiful as Emma would never be interested in someone like me.

"So soft."

"I'm sorry?"

"Erm, your hair." She clears her throat and looks away quickly. "It's so soft."

"Oh. Thanks." Was she blushing?

She starts the water running behind my head and sprinkles some over my hair. "It's not too hot is it?"

"No, it's lovely." I smile at the delicious feeling of her fingers running through my hair.

"It's grown a lot since you were in last."

I hadn't expected her to remember that much detail but I'm really glad she has. It makes me feel a little bit special. But the notion soon flees under the pressure of her fingers working on my scalp. Massaging in shampoo or conditioner, I don't care which; I just don't want her fingers to stop. Ever.

"How's college?"

"S'all right."

"Ah huh. What are you doing again?"

"Chemistry, psychology, maths and physics."

"Blimey. Brain alert." She smiles softly at me, her breasts brush against my arm as she leans over me and I think I whimper. I open one eye a crack to see if I did and she's staring at me with a horrified expression on her face. She isn't. She's humming to herself and I try to make out the tune. It sounds familiar but I can't quite place it. It's nice though.

"And what do you want to do with that little lot, Dani?"

"I'm gonna be a doctor."

"Really?"

I nod. So happy that she's impressed, my heart feels like it's growing inside my chest.

"Don't you need biology to be a doctor?"

"No. They'll teach me all the biology I need at med school. They said chemistry, maths and physics were more important. I've been talking to some junior doctors too and they said that the administrators and selectors like to see variety and try to recruit from a wider pool than just the standard sciences."

"Hence the psychology."

"Exactly." She gets it. How fucking cool is that?

She rinses suds from my hair and wraps the towel around my head. My hair really has grown as the tips peep out from the end of the short towel in a little tuft. She grins when she tweaks it and directs me into a chair that faces a false wall in the centre of the room. It means I'm facing the reception desk, but with a huge mirrored wall in front of me. I can't see bubblegum girl, and there's no one else in the salon. It's not the station she was working at before. Deliberate? I glance at Emma in the mirror as she gathers her combs and clips. I doubt it.

156

"So, Dani, what are you looking for this time?" She slowly unwraps the towel, wraps a gown around me that fastens behind my neck and starts to smooth out the tangles. "Just a trim?"

I can't pull my gaze away from hers as I watch her in the mirror. She cocks her head to one side, obviously questioning my silence.

"Maybe something a little more drastic?"

"What would you suggest?"

She tugs the ends around my face and rests her forearms gently on my shoulders. "Not my hair."

"I know. But I'm looking for expert advice, Emma."

"Well, in that case," she says and turns my face from side to side, examining my profile from all angles. "I think it's perfect just the way it is. There's not a thing that I would change."

The song she'd been humming earlier clicked in my head and I couldn't get rid of it. Bruno Mars, *Just the Way You Are*. Did that mean...? Could it be...? Surely not?

Emma's hand leaves my hair and strokes my chin, my jaw, my cheek. Her eyes glisten and she bites her lower lip. It's adorable. I should say thank you or something, right? But my voice doesn't work. My mouth keeps opening and closing, but nothing comes out. The distance between us seems to shrink. One second she's standing behind me, watching me in the mirror, the next she's angling my head up and to the side as she leans in. Slowly. So slowly. I want her to hurry, certain she's going to kiss me, but I want her to take her time too. In case I'm wrong, I want to enjoy this moment for the rest of my life. Her pink tongue darts out between her lips, wetting them, before retreating. Oh I want to taste it, taste her. Her tongue, her lips, her skin. I want to push my tongue between those coral lips and breathe her inside me. I feel dizzy. I can't get enough air into my lungs as she draws closer and closer.

I memorise every inch of her skin, every line, every pore as she gets even closer. I wonder for a moment how old she is, but she can't be more than a couple of years older than me, and I let the thought drift away. Content to let her lead me where she wants to go.

I close my eyes. I can feel her getting nearer still. The tiny hairs on my skin prickle and rise up to meet her, her scent surrounds me. Cocoa and some sort of fruit, maybe strawberries, with an earthy undertone. Deep and rich, and just so Emma. Elementally her.

And so, so soft. Her lips meet mine so fleetingly I open my eyes to make sure she's really there. Hers are still closed and barely millimetres from me. Her skin is flawless, and I wish my arms weren't covered by the rustling gown. She sighs then covers my mouth again. This time there's more pressure, more hunger, more passion. The hand at my jaw curls around the back of my neck and holds me in place as she deepens the kiss. Her tongue licking at my lips until I open them, desperate to taste the questing muscle.

Bliss? Heaven? All my dreams come true? Well, certainly all the ones I'd been having since I first walked into the salon six months ago and Emma had literally haunted me ever since. Now, she's kissing the living daylights out of me. In the salon. In front of the window. And it seems like she doesn't care. I don't notice her turn the chair to the side but she must have as she straddles my lap and leans in. Her hands cradling my head, sliding down my arms, my back, popping open the press-studs on the gown and finding the hem of my t-shirt. Then skin.

I'm covered in goose bumps, simultaneously shivering and burning under her touch, and I still haven't managed to free my hands to touch her. I long to feel her skin beneath my fingertips. I'd imagined spending hours and hours learning every inch. Every dip and curve, every sweeping plane and tiny crease of her body. I want, no, I *need* to know them all.

She tugs my hair.

"Dani? Hello." Her hands are still beside my chin. "So, just a trim then, darlin'?"

I open my eyes quickly and find her staring at me in the mirror, pulling gently on the tips of my hair. I'm breathing hard, panting, my heart's racing, and my face is pale, even though my cheeks are flushed, and I realise what I've done. What I've been doing. While she was watching me.

Her knowing smile and teasing eyes won't let me delude myself. She knows I'm attracted to her. I'm pretty sure she knows I'd just been daydreaming about her, and right now I just want the floor to open up and swallow me. I have never, and I do mean never, been so embarrassed in my entire life.

Not even when I was ten and my little sister dared me to stand on a plank over a barrel to catapult a bucket up to our tree house like we'd seen on a cartoon and I had to go home with a broken nose and explain how it happened with Lisa laughing so hard she was crying the whole time. Even that wasn't as embarrassing as this.

I could leave, of course. Stand up and walk out of the door. If I did, I'd never be able to come back. I'd never see Emma again, and I'd probably never be able to look at myself in the mirror again either.

"Yeah, just a trim."

Emma works quickly, methodically, and chats easily about everything and nothing. The weather, holidays, work, did I watch The X Factor at the weekend? I can't meet her gaze again and with each passing second I try to let go of my fantasies of Emma. Let's face it, she's never gonna want to go for a drink with someone who's so uncool. I mean I was stupid to even think about it, right? I mean she's gorgeous. Got a good job. Probably has a boyfriend even. No, she was flirting with me. Ha. She was just being friendly, idiot. Stop deluding yourself.

I make up my mind. When I finish here, I won't be coming back. I can't face it. I can't face her. I should've known better.

Eventually she finishes drying my hair and I hand over the cash to bubblegum girl before I pull the door open, mumbling thank you as I do. I can't bring myself to look at her again, or I'll let go of my resolve and make another appointment.

"Wait, Dani, you forgot your coat." Emma pulls it from the peg and holds it out.

"Thanks." I take it from her and try to ignore the shock of feeling her hand brush my own. "Sorry." I yank my jacket up my arms as I push my way out of the salon and manage to step straight into a

159

puddle. "For fuck's sake." I tug the hood around my face and turn toward home.

"Do you think you'll ever get round to it?" Emma asks from somewhere behind me.

I turn around. "Excuse me?"

The rain starts to gather on her hair and eyelashes. "I asked if you think you'll ever get round to it."

"To what?"

"Asking me out." She steps toward me.

Holy fuck. Really? "I...I'm...I don't know what you..."

Emma shakes her head. "Never mind." She turns and steps away, disappointment evident in the droop of her shoulders. It's then I realise that she's taken a huge chance following me. She's obviously nervous too. I can see it in the way she twists the cuffs of her shirt in her hands.

"Emma wait."

She stops but doesn't turn around.

"I'm not sure...I've never asked..." I feel just as foolish as I did earlier, when she caught me daydreaming. She's the woman I haven't been able to get out of my mind and she's here, giving me a chance to do what I've been dreaming of.

She turns her head to look over her shoulder. "Everyone has to start somewhere, Dani."

Her voice is so quiet I almost don't hear her but the words stick in my head. She's right. So what I haven't asked a girl out before? So what I don't have a clue what I'm doing? So what I'm scared and might make a fool out of myself? I might not too. I'll never know if I don't take a chance. I mean seriously, what's the worst thing that could happen? She slaps me and I find a new hairdresser? Barring the slapping bit I was already convincing myself to do that anyway.

Her shirt's soaked so I do the only thing I can think of. I take off my coat and wrap it around her shoulders. I screw up what's left of my courage, dignity, self respect and breathe in deep.

"Can I walk you home later?"

There it is. Nothing fancy. No pledges of undying love like you see in the films, or on telly. No falling to my knees or promising a fancy expensive dinner, just a request. A request for time. Emma's time. Time away from work, time with her alone, to see if there could be something between us. Respectful. Fuck, I'm a boring old fart in a college student's body. I should have asked her to go clubbing...

"I'd like that." Emma smiles. Not the mischievous smile of earlier, or the knowing one that had had me blushing. It was sweet, and kind, and hopeful. She pulls my jacket around her body, burrowing into the warmth. "I'd like that a lot." She leans toward me and kisses my cheek. I'd been right about the smell. Chocolate, and strawberries, and Emma, but softer than I could have ever imagined. I run my hand up her arm. Is it real? Like, really real? I've got to know.

I pinch the skin on the back of my hand. "Ow."

Emma pulls back and frowns at me. "Did I hurt you?"

I shake my head so fast I feel like my brain is rattling inside. "No. No, I needed to be sure this was real."

"Don't do that again." She grasps my hand and rubs her thumb over the small welt then lifts my hand to her lips and kisses the red mark. "This is too perfect to spoil with bruises." Her smile lights up her face. "See you later, Dani." She wiggles her finger at me and taps the back of my hand. "Just the way you are."

I push open the door of the salon for her. "I can't wait."

###

ANDREA BRAMHALL lives in Norfolk with her partner, their two border collies and two cats, running their campsite and hostel to pay the bills and writing down the stories she dreams up.

Andrea is an avid reader and a keen musician, playing the saxophone and the guitar. She is also a recreational diver and takes any opportunity to head to warmer climes for a spot of diving.

Andrea's first novel, Ladyfish, received an Alice B. Lavender Certificate and was runner up in the Rainbow Awards Debut Lesbian Novel of 2013 and Lesbian Novel of the year categories. Her second novel, *Clean Slate*, is the Lambda Literary Award winner for Romance 2013. *Clean Slate* and her third novel, *Nightingale*, have both been named as finalists for the 2014 Rainbow Award Lesbian Contemporary Romance Novel of the year category.

ENCORE
Rain McAlistair

STACEY LOOKED at her e-mail inbox page and frowned. Carol Harris. For some reason that name rang a bell. Her eyes slid across to the subject of the e-mail. "School Reunion," it said. Oh yes. Now she had it. Carol Harris was that girl from school who was always organising things. Stacey opened the e-mail and began to read.

Hello Stacey,

I bet it's a surprise to hear from me. I found you on Facebook and got your email address from there. Thank heavens for modern technology as most of the girls from school are married and have different last names now. I didn't think you had gone down that route somehow!

The reason I'm writing is that the school is having a reunion party to mark us all reaching our half century. (Can you believe we are fifty now?) It's going to be held on the 12th of October at the Cricket Club down the road from the school. You will remember the Cricket Club from all the 18th parties we had there. You and the girls played a good few gigs there too. That brings me to the point.

I've asked loads of people to come to the reunion so far and most have said yes. What we all agree on is that it would be fantastic if Blue Jade could reform, just for the night, and play a few songs. You guys were a big part of everything back then and it would be perfect if you made an appearance. Can you track down the other members and see if they'd be interested? I don't want to rush you but I need a confirmation as soon as possible in order to make all the arrangements.

I do hope life is treating you well. We can catch up on news at the party. E-mail me when you have discussed it with the others and let me know. We are all hoping you can make it happen.

Bye for now,

Carol

She wasn't going of course. But even just reading the name Blue Jade had made her heart beat a little faster. It was both the happiest and saddest time in her life. A time when her life had been so closely linked to Martina's. Blue Jade had been the means by which the two of them had come together. After years of worshipping her from afar, Stacey had used the allure of the band to draw Martina closer. Blue Jade had been the magical spell that Stacey had been looking for. Back then all she had wanted to do was cast a spell over Martina that would bind them together. It had almost worked. It all started with the drumsticks.

Stacey wandered over to the window and looked out. The sheep grazed peacefully in the field. The day was not sunny, but at least it was dry, which was unusual for early April. She knew exactly where the photo was, even though she had not looked at it for a long time. Suddenly she longed to see it again. Stacey quickly re-crossed the room. Opening the drawer she drew out the box of old photographs and quickly sifted through until she found the one of Blue Jade. There they stood, frozen in time, holding their instruments and grinning. Stacey was on the right of the photograph with her guitar. And close beside her, their hips touching, stood Martina. She had drumsticks in her right hand. Her left hand was draped on Stacey's shoulder. Stacey barely saw the other three in the photograph. She walked over to the window again and gazed out, thinking back to the day she had first bought the drumsticks. It was so long ago...

It was 1975 the first day Stacey nervously passed through the gates of Saxon Hall School as a senior school pupil. The collar of her blouse felt stiff and her blazer was too big. She noticed Martina straight away in the playground on that first morning. Martina seemed to stand head and shoulders above everyone else. It wasn't that she was particularly tall, although she was taller than Stacey. She seemed to attract people to her like a magnet.

That first day of school, Martina stood, surrounded by a group of girls, animatedly explaining something whilst waving her arms around and laughing. The girls were laughing too. She had beautiful dark blonde, long, thick hair. It was parted in the centre and always looked neat. Her face was plump with good skin and very deep set eyes which took on a worried look when she was thinking. Her lips were full and she often wore a cheeky smile. She gave an impression of solidity and strength without being masculine in any way.

Stacey was just one more bee drawn to this lovely flower, but she felt in awe of Martina. It was a feeling that never fully left her, even after they became close friends years later. Martina didn't just shine socially. Academically she was brilliant. She came top of the class for almost every subject. It was clear she would go far.

One day, in an English lesson, Martina had to give a talk to the class. Stacey could picture her now, nearly forty years later, as she confidently held everyone's attention. Martina had a very distinctive voice. It was steady and commanding. Stacey could even recall some of the words she chose after all this time. The mind is a funny thing.

For the first three years, Stacey and Martina didn't have much to do with each other although they were in the same class. Martina had a big group of friends and Stacey wasn't all that comfortable in large groups. She was happy to admire Martina from afar.

Things changed slightly after a school trip to Wales. Everyone pushed forward to board the minibus at once and a handful of girls were left standing in the car park with no more seats available. These five girls squashed into the teacher's car and Stacey found herself sitting in the back seat next to Martina. Kathy and Janice also sat in the back with Dara in the front next to the teacher. They were all to become firm friends.

When they stopped for a break in the journey, Stacey sneaked off for a cigarette.

"Could I have one of those?" She turned and saw Martina standing next to her, smiling broadly.

"Oh, yes. I didn't know you smoked." Stacey offered her packet to Martina, who took a cigarette and lit up. They were fifteen and for the rest of that holiday, they bonded and became as close as they ever would.

Martina was as deep as a well. She was like night and day all rolled into one. She had her sunny side where she was sociable and confident talking to people of any age. But she also had a troubled side and at times would withdraw and seem to become very sad. Stacey always approached Martina very tentatively. She was constantly afraid of breaking their friendship, which seemed fragile in a way she couldn't explain.

Dara was bold, brash and was always singing. All five girls were music mad and would crowd round the radio at lunch time listening to the chart run down, making notes of chart positions in their books and recording their favourite hits on very basic cassette recorders.

The five friends would go camping often. Stacey would bring her acoustic guitar and while Dara sang the lead Stacey would harmonise and strum. Janice, Kathy and Martina would join in with the singing. Martina rather fancied herself as a drummer and would always keep the beat, tapping on her thighs with her palms. The girls would go to concerts together and their main topic of conversation was music and bands.

One sunny afternoon, while Stacey was visiting her married sister in the North of England, she happened to walk past a music shop with a drum kit in the window. She wished she could just go in and buy it for Martina. She was aware, somewhere in the far recess of her mind, that she loved Martina and would do anything for her. She couldn't buy the drum kit but she did the next best thing. She bought a pair of drumsticks. She remembered now so clearly the spring in her step as she walked along the high street in her sister's town carrying the drumsticks. She had a smile on her face, picturing Martina's reaction.

"Wow! Oh yessssssss!" The gift was enthusiastically received and Martina posed around school with the drumsticks, beating out rhythms on any piece of furniture that came to hand. Never before had Stacey felt so satisfied to give anyone a gift. She had made her friend happy and it gave her such a buzz.

Stacey was in the garden doing her homework when she had her next marvellous idea. Next door lived a large family and four of the teenaged lads had formed a band. They rehearsed in a room at the back of their house. On this day, Nigel, the drummer was practising. The sound carried to Stacey as she sat writing. Nigel was a nice guy. Might he let Martina have a go on his drums? Nigel said yes. Stacey could barely wait to invite Martina round to play on a real drum kit.

When Martina sat at the kit for the first time, Nigel told her to just go wild and play what she wanted at first. Afterwards, having a beer together in Stacey's garden out of sight of her parents, Martina vowed to get her own kit.

Six months later, Blue Jade was formed. They all had instruments now and had become reasonably accomplished at playing them. Stacey loved being in the band but most of all she loved spending so much time with Martina. They would rehearse mostly in Martina's house because the drum kit was there and wasn't easy to transport. They played covers of the pop songs of the time.

Their first gig was in the youth club and went well. The crowd danced and cheered and the girls in the band had a great time. By the time they were eighteen they could drive themselves around and they began playing more sophisticated gigs.

Stacey had held very deep feelings for Martina for three long years now. They were close, but nothing romantic had ever occurred between them, and Stacey never expected it to. It was still the very early 1980s. Stacey didn't know anyone who was gay. She had a boyfriend whom she did not love but they got on quite well together. What she felt for him was but a drop in the ocean compared to how she felt about Martina. Martina had plenty of male admirers but she had not dated so far.

One hot summer day Martina asked Stacey if she wanted to go for a drive. They drove out into the countryside and stopped at a beautiful old rural church. It was deserted and locked but the key was hanging near the arch shaped oak door. Inside, the sun flooded the church with light through the stained glass windows. Martina slowly walked up the aisle and Stacey followed her.

"I'd like to get married here one day." Martina's words broke the hushed quiet as they stood by the font. She had never before mentioned any relationships in her life. She appeared to Stacey like a solitary ship charting a course on an uncertain sea. She still seemed to have many moments of sadness. Stacey felt Martina had many secrets that she would never know about.

As they explored the church in awed silence, Stacey wanted to take Martina's hand and tell her just how she felt. She wanted to tell her that she loved her, had loved her for years. She wanted to ask her to stay with her always. But the words wouldn't come. She was too afraid. She wanted to stop time right there and then. It was a perfect moment and she never forgot it.

Not long afterwards, they drifted apart, as most school friends do, amidst the busy lives they were all building now they were going to work or university. Stacey moved away and married. Very unhappily as it turned out. But she finally struggled out of the restrictions of the heterosexual lie she had been leading to a very happy new life. She was never able to forget Martina though or shake free from the spell she had cast on her the first day she saw her.

Now here she was, fifty years old, and somewhere out there in the world was Martina. What sort of life had she led? Was she married? Was she happy? Was there any chance at all that Martina had ever felt something for her? Stacey still played the guitar. She was frightened to seek out Martina and yet, having cast her mind back to those far off days, she now knew she would do the reunion concert if it meant a chance to see her again.

With her stomach doing flip flops she began to think who she could call to get the numbers for any of the old Blue Jade members. Finally she traced Nadine who had been at school with them and had been quite close to Dara. Nadine had a number for Dara and with trembling hands Stacey punched in the numbers and waited to hear her old friend's voice for the first time in so many years.

"Stacey! How brilliant to hear from you. How ARE you?" Dara's voice sounded just the same - bubbly and enthusiastic.

"I'm fine. I heard from Carol Harris and was wondering if any of you are into doing this reunion gig?"

Dara's voice fell. "Ah well I don't think it would be the same without Martina, do you?"

"Oh, does she not want to do it then?" Stacey tried to hide her disappointment.

"Oh God, Stacey. Have you not heard?"

"Heard what?"

"Martina died, in January of this year. I'm so sorry; I assumed you knew."

There was a long pause. Then finally, "No. I didn't know."

"Yes it was so sad."

After another long pause, Stacey managed to speak again.

"Do you happen to know where she is buried, Dara?"

"Saint Bartholomew's Church. I've been myself. It's a lovely spot."

They said their goodbyes and Stacey ended the call.

A quick look on the internet confirmed what Stacey had guessed. The churchyard where Martina lay was the place they had visited over thirty years ago on that perfect summer day.

The churchyard had changed very little considering how much time had passed. Stacey went inside the church and said a prayer first. She carried her flowers outside and soon found the place. There was no headstone yet. Just a simple cross with the name on it.

She stood for a long time remembering Martina's grinning face as she beat out a rhythm on her drum kit. Stacey did not think of Martina's sad moments. They had been as close as Martina would allow, maybe as close as the era they grew up in would allow. Anything more was not to be. She placed the flowers on the grave, took a last look and walked away. Nestled in the bouquet lay a pair of drumsticks. A last gift to one who was adored.

###

RAIN MCALISTAIR was born in Warwickshire, England in 1962 and now lives on the West Coast of Ireland. She has written four books of modern lesbian romantic fiction. Her first book, *Dove* was published in 2010. She has since written *Bridge*, *Moonchaser* and *Leaving*. Rain shares her home with her partner and a large lurcher, a timid English pointer and a very vocal cat. She relaxes by playing the guitar, bass and drums and loves old black and white films.

Website: www.rainmcalistair.com

Links to books

www.amazon.co.uk/Dove-their-dream-survive-against/dp/1456420135/
www.amazon.co.uk/Bridge-Rain-McAlistair/dp/1468177796/
www.amazon.co.uk/Moonchaser-Rain-McAlistair-ebook/dp/B00956VY8M/
www.amazon.co.uk/Leaving-Rain-McAlistair/dp/1491025417/

THE WAITING GAME
Katie Bennett-Hall

MAGGIE SAW the brunette that night when the usual crowd were meeting at a bar. Nothing out of the ordinary, but the brunette was there, as always. Maggie was (un)consciously ecstatic to see her, working hard to disguise the feelings so that neither the brunette, nor anyone else would notice on the pleasantly warm Wednesday evening in June.

The usual crowd had gathered, the cocktail menu on special – threatening risky behaviour later. Maggie was off work for the week, so settled in to let her hair down without having to worry about the morning after suffering.

She talked with some friends and went to buy a round of drinks. On her return from the bar, the brunette entered the venue and made a beeline straight for her. Maggie's heart skipped a beat. She took a slow deep breath to keep it from pulsing too fast. The brunette joined in the casual conversation at the table. Maggie made the tiresome effort to show the right amount of balance, bringing the brunette into the group, but paying equal attention to everyone at the table.

Seven months before, Maggie had received the knockback message from the brunette. They had both entered a space where something happening between them had become a real possibility. Maggie had just ended the nightmare of rebound relationships. The brunette, it seemed hopeful for once, had left her difficult and emotionally draining long-term relationship.

They'd been out at a night, bowling with the usual crowd. They'd spent the evening furiously flirting in between turns; it had become so much the norm that no-one really paid attention anymore. It was harmless and just reflected the fact that Maggie and the brunette had history; a secret history that the whole of the usual crowd knew about.

Towards the end of that night, Maggie had made it clear she intended on more than flirting. They'd already had lunch together that day, one of the many inappropriate activities they shared that only they knew about. Maggie sat patiently listening to how serious the brunette finally was about leaving this time...the brunette had "had enough" of "making the effort to make it work" for the previous two and a half years.

Maggie and the brunette were sitting close together on the plastic Super Bowl chairs, and a jolt of electricity hit them both as their thighs, quite deliberately, brushed up against each other. Maggie drew a breath and said, "I still think of you, you know."

The brunette paused and said, "I didn't know that. Thank you."

The brunette broke away from the gaze they'd been holding. "It's time for us to leave," she said. "I just need to use the ladies' first." Maggie put on her coat and scarf and processed what that meant. When the brunette returned, she was already dressed to leave. She turned to Maggie and said, "Thank you for what you said. I really had no idea. But I think we are better as friends." Maggie sagged as though the brunette had taken a safety pin and pierced her heart, but forced a smile and replied, "Yes, ok. Your friendship is very important to me."

On the way home, Maggie berated herself to the core for the mistake she had made, putting her feelings out there like that. She fidgeted while processing the revelation that if it couldn't happen now, when they were both pretty much single and available, it probably never would.

It was the kick up the arse Maggie needed to move on from the past and to downgrade her expectations to fond thoughts of the time the two women had enjoyed together two years before, rather than waste her efforts and her life away with the hope of recapturing it.

So, Maggie thought it only fair to give the brunette equal attention at the bar and ignore the fact that her bones ached for the beautiful woman whenever they were in the same vicinity.

The brunette, however, had other plans on that warm June evening. She gracefully, artfully drew Maggie into a conversation for just the two of them. Maggie found it impossible to resist and relinquished her full attention to the brunette, quickly becoming unaware of anyone else around her. Soon it was time to buy more drinks, and Maggie was quick to offer, satisfying their shared passion for cocktails. Those were quickly inhaled and the brunette was next to the bar.

This gave Maggie a moment to emerge from her daze and notice the crowd around her. A pretty blonde she had not seen before was chatting loudly and happily to some of the others. Maggie caught the blonde's eye, and a smile in the process. She took the opportunity to break from the futile fog where she'd spent the last hour. Moving to the new table, finding just one space for herself, Maggie seamlessly joined in with the banter. The brunette returned with Maggie's drink in hand and passed it on silently.

Maggie relaxed and enjoyed the laughter with the new person and caught herself beginning to flirt and be flirted with. Someone else from the table stood up and immediately the brunette squeezed in, sitting down next to Maggie, next round of cocktails already in hand, demanding Maggie's attention. Maggie did not allow herself to be distracted this time and continued flirting with the blonde. The conversation around the table was full of jokes and laughter.

Maggie started to tell a very animated tale, waving her arms about in excited gesture. Coupled with the cool summer's breeze from the open doors, and unbeknown to Maggie, this triggered an uncontrollable sensual awakening in the brunette.

The brunette, Christina, breathed in the intoxicating scent of Maggie, who was obliviously telling an elaborate tale of stupidity or bad behaviour. Christina sat back and gazed at Maggie, zoning in and out of listening to the story, all her senses full through vision and aroma.

Christina could barely stand the intensity of desire she suddenly felt and wondered from where it arose. Silly question, she realised; it had always been there ever since the accidental-illicit-exquisitely-romantic fling two and a half years ago. Most of the time Christina had acclimatised to suppressing the curious feelings and reactions in the belief that she was "doing the right thing" and continuing to work on the relationship she thought she deserved.

In the meantime, Christina and Maggie's friendship had flourished, and moments of inappropriateness and impropriety were dealt with through humour. Although Christina, in these moments of adulterous humour, winced with pain recalling her second romantic rejection of Maggie.

Declaring she thought they were better "just as friends", Christina was hiding that she was not yet brave enough to risk such an important and dear friendship through all the drama becoming a couple would bring. Instead Christina had maintained a safe enough distance from Maggie. A safe enough distance from the truth of her feelings, maintaining control of the situation; despite sensing the chemistry every time Maggie walked into the room; and despite knowing Maggie had once, at least, felt the same way. So, what exactly made it all rise up to the unsafe surface on this random, routine mid-summer night?

Christina noticed Maggie was finishing her drink and used the opportunity to escape to the bar and away from the temptation. Returning with the cocktails, she decided to use the only thing that worked in these situations, humour. Awaiting a helpful pause in conversation, Christina seized her chance. "What perfume are you wearing?" (She was desperate to know).

"Oh, just the new Calvin Klein thing. Why?" Maggie replied.

"It is really strong! Let me smell." Christina grabbed Maggie's arm and drew in a deep breath.

"Let me too," said the blonde, who Christina was finding terribly tiresome.

Soon everyone was smelling Maggie's arm and laughing which would normally have been enough to let Christina start suppressing the feelings again.

"Stop waving your arms around when you talk; your perfume is too strong," Christina said.

Maggie recalled only dabbing on a little that evening. She had been excited about all the sexy women sniffing her arm, especially the blonde, – who sadly had to leave to make the last train home. Maggie was blocked in and could not get out to give the blonde a hug goodbye or her number. She waved instead and then leaned back and rested her arm on the chair backs either side of her.

She realised she had been drinking strong cocktails all evening and was on the verge of being very drunk. Time to go home she thought. She stood up and went to grab her purse then turned to Christina who was leaning back on the chair next to her also looking like she had enjoyed one cocktail too many. "I'm going home," Maggie said. "Nearly the last train."

"Oh, ok," said Christina, standing up as well. "I'll go with you; I think we can get the same train."

"Sure" replied Maggie, thankful for the company on the tedious walk to the station. Saying goodbyes to all took its usual time and other people started to make moves to leave.

"Let's hurry," Christina said, rushing them out before they could be joined. "We can probably make the next one." Walking at a pace, Christina asked Maggie what story she had been telling whilst Christina was buying drinks. Maggie started to recount, and her arms were quick to become a part of the narrative again. Christina stopped Maggie and walked to stand the other side of her.

"What are you doing?" asked Maggie.

"The breeze is blowing your perfume downwind. It's really strong."

"Sorry I didn't realise" said Maggie, apologetically.

"No, it's not that," replied Christina. "I...like it".

Maggie said "Oh," then realised the significance of the unexpected remark. "Oh! Ok."

"Yes, so stop waving your arms around."

"Yes, right. Sorry."

They continued walking and talking towards the station. As they approached the station concourse, it became clear there was only a minute to make the train. Christina was in high stiletto heels and sighed at the thought of running for the train. Maggie grabbed hold of her hand, determined to make it. They ran and swiped their Oyster cards simultaneously through the barrier. Still holding hands they boarded the train. Breathless, they sat down on two seats facing each other.

Reluctantly, Maggie dropped Christina's hand. She had four station stops' worth of time left with Christina, holding onto the high at Christina's earlier reaction and declaration. After months of convincing herself she had moved on, accepting that there would never be the relationship she had wished for so long, she was suddenly confused. She hadn't had a response acknowledging anything physical between them for nearly two years.

Christina felt an unwanted and guilty disappointment when Maggie dropped her hand. She knew how wrong it was, still in a relationship, albeit finally ready to leave. Yet, at that moment she wanted nothing more than for Maggie to lean forward and kiss her. The minutes until the train arrived at her station sped by far too quickly, and after what seemed like only seconds, her stop was being called out by the automated train announcer.

Christina stood up slowly, looking at Maggie. "Well, bye then," Christina said, filled with hope, every inch of her silently desperate for Maggie to stand up, take her in her arms and kiss her with the passion of two years' bottled up desire. But Maggie stayed seated and said, "Goodbye," with a wave and hint of a smile that masked all of the energy it was taking not to stand up and pull Christina into her.

As Christina disembarked from the train, a tear formed in Maggie's eye. Had she missed her opportunity? Was the chemistry still there on both sides, or were her own feelings blinding the interpretation of Christina's behaviour? She filled with regret that conflicted with hope. Had Christina given her a sign?

Full of fear, Maggie took out her phone and typed a text message. She longed to write about her regret at not standing up and kissing Christina. Instead, she drafted:

Had a great night. Fancy dinner tomorrow, at mine?

Ambivalently suggestive and innocent, deflecting culpability. The reply came as quickly as it could have been typed.

Love to.

###

KATIE BENNETT-HALL is a thirty-something journalist and writing lesbian Londoner. She is co-founder and editor of the Planet London and Planet Brighton websites, alongside her wife. In the few spare minutes of the day she is not working or playing Candy Crush, she can be found writing or at least thinking about it. A poet since the age of 5, creative writing cup winner at high school, writing is all she ever wanted to do.

NEW YORK, NEW YES
Chloe A Marshall

THE TRAIN THRUMS along the lines, people neatly lined along the seats in silence. Expressionless, travelling to somewhere, anywhere but here. Some read a book, some a newspaper, others fiddle with their phones while one, there's always one, casts a roaming gaze across the carriage.

I pull my skirt down and shield one arm across my chest in defence. Nothing to see here. Move along. If only. Seems like I'm invisible in my baggy jeans and vest, but the minute I'm feminine I'm also fair game. I look right at him. He suddenly locks his view into the middle of nowhere, vacant, quickly fixing the appropriate focus onto precisely nothing.

The doors open at the stop for Brooklyn Museum. A new one sits down beside me. Elbows overbearing, legs spread, no concept of personal space. Movement towards me, so close I can smell his breath. Eyes darting, body shifting, asshole attitude prevailing. The anger and the subway heat rise in me as I begin to sweat.

The daily commute in this city must be a bland, blank sheet of dullness, only to be punctuated by the stabbing eyes of nuisance voyeurs. I'm either perved at or I simply don't exist. And I'm only doing this, donning this femme drag, for you. The one person on this planet who I actually want to know that I'm alive and kicking. I hope you notice it; I hope you appreciate it.

I pass the crowds in a blur, stunted beneath the massive skyscrapers that I'm still getting used to. I keep moving and follow signs for the aptly named Meatpacking District – both a red light and a gay area.

I take a deep breath and a quick look at my reflection in the blacked out window. My make-up is already smeared in the searing sunshine and smog, but even so I wish I'd opted for jeans instead of a skirt. I hope I don't seem like some bi-curious gal who's just looking for an experiment: that would be embarrassing.

But I'm in a new place looking for new adventure, so it's about time I check out this tacky, sleazy dive. With a final glance at the sprawling skyline and the wide, endless traffic-filled streets, I descend the stairs into a dingy basement. Set below a sex shop, the garish red neon sign simply says Bar, sitting atop crumbly black paint that covers the entire exterior of the building. But the little rainbow flag next to the lurid sign does reassure me somewhat.

It's not my first time in a gay bar, but it is my first time while being underage in the US. I'm not sure how this place will compare to a haze of drunken, sloppy snogs to the tinny, poppy soundtrack of the piss poor London university LGBT night.

Five dollars in the palm of a transvestite's hand and I'm in, relieved to be out of the relentless crowds and heat. Leathered skinheads prop up the bar, while some younger guys sport clingy t-shirts and trousers, milling around the dingy dancefloor in synch to the pumping techno beat. Mirrored disco balls send flashes of light around the small space, illuminating the dark, seedy setting of where I hope to find someone in the shadows. Meerkat-like glances are constantly being exchanged but with such loud music, hardly any words.

The separate single sex toilets catch my eye – if there are provisions for ladies then I can't have got it entirely wrong. All the cubicles are empty though: no sign of female life here whatsoever. I catch myself by surprise in the mirror, with my weirdly defined blue eyes and overly big and shiny lips standing out more than I'd like. Looks like a toddler has got an artist's brush and pallet and haphazardly blobbed over any random parts of me that will take the colour. The slap does make me look older though, so much so that I didn't get ID'd despite being a few months shy of twenty one.

I smooth down my frizzy bleached blonde hair and reapply my lipstick for something to do and try to summon up the courage to head to the bar. A quick bump of white powder will soon help with that, I think, as I make the most of my solitary moment and chop, cut and sniff. May as well grab a drink; maybe the leathermen will be able to enlighten me about New York's hidden lesbian hangouts.

I sink into a barstool, smile at the topless barman and drink my beer. What the hell am I doing here? But the question melts out of my mind as I focus on the music, with the volume somehow increasing in my head until I can hear nothing else. The fast rhythm is sending my thoughts in a spin, the vibrating baseline reverberating through my entire body. My face pulsates and the rush hits me, and nothing else matters as I'm numb yet overwhelmed with pleasure.

I watch as tall torsos dance in unison, their sweat and energy sucking me in. My head nods to the beat and for one strange moment I imagine that I'm a guy too. I have a boyish baby face to contrast with my broad, bulging muscles. Oh, and a massive throbbing cock of course. I laugh to myself like a madwoman. I wonder how it feels to fuck or be fucked with one, to have a part of me that bulges in my trousers, growing into a stiff new shape whenever I'm excited.

All of a sudden I snap out of the daydream, looking up to see the vague outline of a buxom figure. She's tall, broad and bulky, even among a room full of men. With no airs or graces, she pushes past the cross dresser on the door who fires her a sour, scathing look in return. Flashing the stamp on her hand, she marches in and manically scans the space. Thudding across the room on heavy platform goth boots, she's all buckles and chains that glisten in the disco lights. She catches my eye pretty quickly and holds my gaze, making a beeline straight for me. Shit.

"You're new," she brashly announces in her elongated American drawl. Staring at me intently, seemingly unaware of how predatory and obvious she's being. Her dark, heavily lined eyes pierce directly into mine, revealing a confidence and directness with no let up. I shuffle on my stool. She knows I'm nervous, but she also knows what I want. It's like she can read my mind.

I say nothing back, already pissed off at being made to feel even more self-conscious than I already had been. It's hard to shake off the nerves, my stomach in knots as I wonder what this gobby, thirty something sadist wants with me. I'd finally found the confidence to step foot in this place, but I'm not sure if I'm really ready for this, or her.

She clicks her fingers obnoxiously to be served a beer. As she lifts her drink, I notice her arms are solidly covered with tattoos and as she steps towards me I'm still not sure if she's trying to seduce me or intimidate me. Standing in front of me now, she rests a big inked arm on the bar and effectively blocks my escape route. Great.

Her large chest is puffed up and right in my face, and I try not to stare. A leather corset placed over her dress somehow breaks up the bulges, pulling in slightly at the middle and leading up to her ample cleavage. I wonder what such a substantial pair would feel like in my hands, or mouth. All I've really known is the cute little tits that perch perfectly on my petite frame.

Her tight-fitting black mini dress doesn't do much to conceal her bulky body, her legs almost as wide as they are long. With fat bulging out of her ripped fishnet tights, I quite admire the fact that she feels no need to conceal her hefty weight. Somehow her big body fits perfectly with her big personality.

She takes a few big gulps of her beer, peering down at me as she swallows. "So, what's your name princess?" Sweeping a lock of long jet-black hair behind one ear, she attempts a fake smile with her thin, unappealing lips. When I don't reciprocate, she slams down the bottle and sighs.

"Um, Kate," I reply, feeling shy but trying my best to conceal it. "Oh my God, you're British aren't you? Wow! My father is from England. He drinks tea, like, all the time. I bet you do too. He'd love you!" she says, looking me up and down and weirding me out with thoughts of her imaginary dad doing the same.

"Look, sorry, I'm not really... Well, y'know." I have no clue how to let this large, scary woman down softly.

"What? Not a big ol' dyke? Come on, of course you are. Let's get out of here." And with that, she downs the rest of her drink and slides her big hand around my small waist. But instead of recoiling, I feel a surge of electricity upon her touch, a spark that for some reason makes me want more. Truth is, a small part of me can't ignore the curiosity that she incites in me. She knows it, too, as she lays claim to me and proudly marches me out of the bar.

Daylight dazzles me as I'm reminded of the outside world in which normal people go about their day. Suited men pass swiftly, looking away from us in fear of their little minds being blown by what we might be doing. She puts on her shades and looks so cool, like she really, genuinely doesn't give a fuck what anyone thinks. I blindly follow her across the parking lot towards her truck, with shaking, jelly like legs. I'm terrified, but I'm too excited to care.

I accidentally get in the driver's seat, embarrassingly, as she laughs at me yet again for my quaint Britishness. I switch sides and then she gets in, cranking up Slipknot to full volume and promptly sliding her free hand up my skirt. Feeling relieved that she's driving an automatic, I'm still unnerved as she slams her foot down hard on the accelerator. Speeding down the freeway, she begins to explore my body as if she already owns it.

Placing her hand on my inner thigh, she pushes my legs open. I knew I'd spread them for her anyway, but ready or not she takes what she wants. Running her hand over my knickers and then rubbing her knuckles up and down the outline of my slit, she continues until the dampness passes through the material and onto her hand. I try to subtly readjust my skirt. There's no point in saying anything: she'd never hear. I just hope that none of the passing truck drivers are looking down, enjoying a full view of our antics.

"Act all coy, but you're so fucking wet!" she laughs, as we pull up to the driveway of wherever the hell she's taking me. She cuts the engine and kills the music. "I bet you taste fucking good too." She raises an eyebrow as if it's a question. "Don't you?" She shoves her fingers in my mouth. "Don't you," she says, more forcefully this time. I lick and suck on the fingers that have just been groping me, grabbing me, touching me. As she penetrates my mouth and makes me taste my own juices, I think about how our lips have never even met to kiss. I don't even know her name.

"So, do you often make a habit of going home with strangers then? Bet you do. Bet you're underage, too. Don't worry, I know your type. I know what to do with girls like you." She smirks. All I'd done is follow her lead, yet here she is talking to me like some little slut. No doubt she'd had her fair share, but I'd barely got two words in edgeways, let alone put myself on a plate for her.

I shift in my seat. "What do you mean, 'girls like me'?"

"You've no right to ask questions," she barks. "You tell me – you know what I mean. Don't be naive."

I hesitate as she glares at me, impatient for an answer to my evidently stupid question. "Um, am I a little slut?" I ask tentatively. And as the words fall out my mouth, I'm all the more aroused for the filth of it all.

"Yes, yes you are. But since you've phrased that as a question, I'm gonna gag you until you've learnt your lesson." She yanks off my sodden knickers and shoves them into my mouth. "Understand?" I nod, the only form of communication I have left. "Plus – you're only half right. You're not a little slut. You're my little slut."

She finally unlocks the car doors and gets out of the car. I instinctively follow as she makes her way to the back entrance of a huge detached house that's surrounded by tall trees. I'm relieved that no prying eyes can see as I walk in, head down, pants in my mouth.

I find myself in a pitch-black building, hearing nothing but the sound of her slamming and locking the door. Keys are turned, bolts are fastened and padlocks are clicked into place. When she's finally finished locking up, all I can hear is the sound of my own body. My beating heart feels like it's in my mouth, along with my heavy breathing which is getting faster and faster as I try not to panic. There's no way I can escape from this, and nobody else knows I'm here.

I want to walk around but when she places one firm hand on my stomach and one on my back I know to stand still. "Arms out," she says simply. All I can do is give her what she wants. She unhooks the back of my bra, pulling the straps down and sliding it out of the side of my top. My nipples feel extra sensitive against the fabric. "That's better, no underwear at all." I can almost see her smile as she makes her observations. "Arms up." And with that, she uses my bra to tie my wrists together, connecting them to some kind of hook on the ceiling.

"Spread them, slut." And I do, as she ties a leather cuff around each ankle, hooking them to a long metal bar that she places in between. She tugs on the restraints and checks that everything is secure and tells me to wait there – not that I have much choice. I listen carefully to the sound of her big black boots as she stomps across the hard wooden floor, until the rhythmic sound gradually trails off and eventually disappears.

Still in total darkness and silence, I have no clue how much time has passed but all I know is that I'm dripping wet with arousal, my mind racing with the many ways in which I want to be fucked. I'm breathing deeply and rhythmically moving my hips back and forth, just thinking about it. And the worst part is that I can't say a word; I can't shout out to her because I've got this delicious and ever frustrating specimen in my mouth. Yes, I'll admit it. I love the smell and taste of myself but I don't need to be gagged with this very symbol of cunt loving narcissism to be reminded that, yes, I am indeed a 'big ol' dyke'.

She's been gone for ages. If she's done this deliberately to instil fear and anticipation then it's bloody well working. I make a muffled noise, realising at once how pathetic I sound. "Hello?" I try to say. My garbled mumbles make no sense. "Is anybody there?" Silence. Then eventually, footsteps. Pacing and laughing.

"I've been watching you on night vision CCTV this entire time, wondering how long you'd take." She's right in my face, a booming voice to make me jump.

"Are you ready then?" She raises an eyebrow. "I'll assume those silly noises were you telling me that you're finally ready." I nod. "I need to hear you say it though." Ripping the pants out of my mouth, she allows me to utter one final word. Her hand cups my chin as I'm forced to look up and face her. "Just say the word sweetheart... Just say 'Yes'." Inhale, exhale. I peer into those deep, dark eyes and feel a weakness from within. I don't know if it's love, lust, submission or sheer curiosity that makes me do it. But my mind is awash with fantasies and my body is aching with desire, and it's as if I have no choice. I whisper my one word affirmative and give myself to her willingly.

"Ok, great. From now on, call me Mistress. But only speak when you're spoken to." She blindfolds me and then flicks on the lights, but I still can't see a thing. "Understood?"

I nod. "Yes." She slaps me hard, right in the face. I gasp as the stinging sensation burns across my cheek and ear, only to feel my face redden further with embarrassment.

"Yes what?" she booms.

"Yes Mistress," I concede.

"You've got a lot to learn. Incompetent little blonde bitch." I stand in silence, wary of saying or doing the wrong thing. I can feel her body close to mine and I arch my back, trying to get closer. "I'm sure you agree, don't you slave?" she purrs in my ear, sending shivers down my spine. Angry in one moment and seductive the next, I can never tell what she's thinking.

"Yes Mistress, please teach me Mistress. I beg you."

The blindfold tightens at the back of my head, and she pulls on it teasingly. "Do you think you deserve to have this removed yet?" I don't know. Shit. If I say yes, I might be scolded for arrogance but if I say no, she may agree and keep it on.

"Up to you Mistress, you know best." It's soon whipped off and I squint as my eyes adjust, finally able to take in my surroundings.

"I kept it on 'til now as I didn't wanna scare you off when we first arrived. I'm pretty sure this would have been too much too soon."

Chains hang from wall to wall, dark hues of purple and red adorn the walls and I can see lots of strange metal objects with hooks, restraints and cuffs connected to them. A tall wooden frame looks like it could be used to tie a standing person to the many hooks, along with a sex swing and stirrups that hang off the centre. A human-size cage stands next to a chair with a cross at the back and wide open leg panels instead of a seat. A large black wooden cross is fixed to the wall, along with a rack that displays an endless collection of whips, crops, paddles and canes. Tall glass cabinets house many small, intricate metal and glass items that I guess are designed to clamp, squeeze and penetrate. Looks like there may be some knives, scalpels and needles in there too. I notice some gas masks, pipes and air tanks in the corner and wonder how they might be used, and I realise how little I really know about all this.

But the most surprising sight of all is my Mistress. She relaxes on her lavish velvet throne, in a new outfit which takes my breath away. Her skintight catsuit shows off the curves of her body, but not an inch of skin. Thigh-high black leather boots grip against those strong, sizeable thighs and end with an elegant pointed toe and metal stiletto high heel. Her dark smokey eyes and black lips are utterly captivating, enhanced by her long jet-black hair, which is pulled back into a high pony tail. The full-length leather gloves match her boots, covering her hands and arms so that only her striking face is fully visible.

My arms ache as they've been tied above me for hours, but I don't mind. In fact I like the idea of suffering for her and realise that I'm ready to do a lot more than this to please her. She uncrosses her long legs, gets up and walks towards me, and I feel myself tense up in her presence. Glossy straightened hair falls down her back, swishing from side to side as she moves, her big breasts bouncing and nipples jutting out with a pronounced outline against the thin material. I don't dare look between her legs and can only imagine the beauty of what's there too. Her hips sway as she paces the room, wearing her stilettos with elegance and ease.

"Glad I let you take a look?" Those dark eyes stare at me, intimidating me as I struggle to find the right words.

"Yes Mistress, thank you. You look beautiful, really." She waves off my comment.

"Just remember what adjective you've used. Each compliment must be distinct. If you can't be creative, you can't stay." I quickly run a list of appropriate words through my mind and realise that none of them are really adequate. She places a leather covered hand over my face until I can no longer breathe, not taking it away until I start to struggle. "Everything that you see, hear and breathe is a privilege. A gift from me to you. I can take away your air or any of your senses at any time I like, especially when you misbehave. Just you remember that slave." I wonder if I'll ever be allowed to touch her or taste her, but I don't dare to ask. These are privileges that must be earned.

"Ok, let's see what we've got." Her eyes dart up and down my body, scrutinising me. I feel vulnerable in my short shirt and top, with no underwear to preserve whatever tiny shred of dignity I may have left. My tits stick forward as I hang on my arms, with my arse also up high thanks to the heels I'm wearing. I know my inner thighs are dripping wet, having stood here for so long with a throbbing, aching pussy that's in dire need of attention.

She grabs my top and pulls it up above my head, revealing my bare boobs. She smiles, grabbing them with both hands. "Nice little round ones, pert and firm like I'd expect from a young slut like you." I gasp as she increases the pressure of her grip, surprised by the sensation of her hard touch against the soft leather on her hands. "Those cute pink nipples look pretty tasty too." She helps herself to my body, sucking and licking my nipples and even giving them a gentle bite. Black lipstick marks the outline of my nipples and my skin is already red from her grip, but that doesn't stop her for a second.

"Pretty toned and slim in general, I see." She runs her hands across my stomach, up and down my back and over my bum. "Looks good. The skinny bitches always suffer the most though." She laughs, while I wish I had more padding. Standing behind me now, she gives me a good, hard spank. I let out a little moan. My buttocks feel raw but the sensation shoots right up between my legs, reverberating over my lips and clit. Fuck that feels good. I want more but I'm too afraid to ask.

Circling me, I feel as if I'm being inspected like a whore in a brothel as she looks me up and down yet again. "Ass out, slut." As I edge backwards, she pulls my skirt up and reveals yet another part of me. "That's it, now lean forwards." I gasp with excitement, enjoying the feeling of exposing myself, feeling like she's objectifying every inch of my body. "Great ass too: just as tight as your titties." Leering over me, she stands behind me and firmly grabs my ass even though it still stings from the spanking. My ass cheeks are putty in her hands as she digs her fingers into them and makes me yelp with pleasure yet again. "Hmmm, let's have a better look down here. Bend over for Mistress, you filthy whore." And as I do so, I realise my cunt is fully exposed from behind and that those grabbing hands are now pulling my cheeks apart.

Air rushes onto my sticky pussy, making me even more sensitive as I feel her roaming eyes take in my most intimate parts. "Very nice, I must say. Someone's excited. You're dripping down your thighs though, how desperate and undignified." I wonder if she'll touch me there, or whether she'll just keep me hanging, literally, until she thinks I deserve it. I keep quiet for a while as she continues to inspect me. "Juicy clit, perfectly positioned between those swollen pussy lips. I wonder how deep that hole of yours can be fucked. And then there's your asshole, of course. Don't think that will be ignored."

She continues grabbing me and opening me up, peering into my every orifice yet not making any direct contact. I can't take it any longer. "Please Mistress..." I whimper. "Permission to speak Mistress?" She stops for a moment and stands tall in front of me.

"Well well, how bold. Think you've got something to say? Better be important as I am not a patient woman. Fine – get your little missive over with!" I feel really stupid now, wishing I'd kept my mouth shut rather than interfering.

"Um, I just wanted to say that you're welcome to touch me..." I hesitate and hang my head to the floor. "Everywhere". Mistress looks at me, bemused for a moment, and then shakes her head.

"You can't give me what's already mine."

Sighing, the Mistress takes a selection of whips, paddles and floggers off the wall and tells me I need to be taught a lesson. Finally unhooking me, she allows me one brief moment to shake my arms and legs, only to be instructed "Strip!" and I drop my top and skirt to the floor. "Crawl, don't walk. Know your place – on the floor, beneath me." I kneel naked at her feet as she fastens a collar around my neck. A chain is connected and then as she gets up Mistress whistles and her bitch follows on the lead. I worry that I'll not be able to satisfy her, that I'll not be able to take the pain properly. She pulls me up and leans me over a low table and roughly ties me down to keep me on my hands and knees. "Doggy position, perfect." I can't move, not an inch.

The hot, hard hand hits me as she spanks, rhythmically. "Ahh... Ohhh... Thank you Mistress." Electrical surges build as my buttocks glow, as she hits me in the same place over and over and the discomfort increases. I imagine her touch on my pussy, while the pain and pleasure find their own way around my body. She must think I'm ready for more, as she moves on to a flogger with long tassels that send slight stinging sensations across my ass, thighs and back. I attempt to raise my bum higher and open my legs wider, to subtly show her what I want. Then I feel one hard thud between my legs. Red hot pain takes over. I scream and collapse onto the table, trying to get my breath back.

"Ooops, I just whipped your pretty pussy." A huge rush of adrenaline kicks in, and the hurting turns into healing. I can hear myself breathe deeply and moan as if I'm about to climax, but I feel like I'm not really present. Flashes of euphoria carry me away, and I have no self-control as the waves of ecstasy are released from my throbbing clit and my G spot deep inside. The whipping continues, this time deliberately right on my cunt, as tears fall from my eyes and I elevate to a higher state of consciousness. I can no longer hear, see or connect to reality – she'd warned me about this. All I can do is feel, and it's the most intense feeling in the world as I scream, convulse and cum in the most amazing orgasm of my life.

I hear the whip drop to the ground, and the metal heels clatter across the floor towards me. My heart is pounding frantically. She strokes my hair back and kisses my sweaty forehead. I smile up at her, still lightheaded. "You look exhausted. You deserve a break. Let's go lie down." I concur.

"Thank you, thank you for everything. Well worth wearing a skirt for." She gently removes the rope and I'm finally free to move.

"My pleasure. We've got the place for twenty four hours, so that was just the beginning... Wait and see what else I've got planned!"

She uncorks a bottle of Champagne and pours me a glass, handing it to me in an elegant long stemmed glass. "Here you go beautiful." She winks. As I take it she glances at my wrists. The skin looks chafed and raw: it'll probably bruise. "Sorry love, that rope is a bit rough."

"It's fine," I smirk. I like it rough. "It's a gift to be marked by you," I say, rubbing over it and not wanting the stinging, tantalising reminder of this moment to ever end.

###

CHLOE A MARSHALL Ever since she learnt the alphabet, Chloe has been writing stories. She's now a freelance journalist and sub editor, contributing to Diva magazine, g3 magazine, the Guardian and the Huffington Post.

Chloe loves to write women's fiction, contemporary romance, queer fiction and adult literotica, always incorporating strong female protagonists, strange subcultures and dark psychological themes. She's the author of many a smutty short story, published by House of Erotica books. She's currently working on her first novel, which she hopes to finish in 2015.

Her three favourite things are words, women and shoes.

You can find out more here: chloeamarshall.org.uk

ACKNOWLEDGEMENTS

A huge thank you to all of the wonderful authors who took the time to submit a story. And an even huger thank you to our editor, Jayne Fereday, who has worked tirelessly to bring this anthology together.

R U COMING OUT

Coming out can be really hard. It's a complicated process which often causes feelings of confusion, doubt, guilt, shame, excitement, fear, relief and anxiety. There is no rule book explaining the best way or time to tell your loved ones that you are gay, lesbian or bisexual. That's because there is no 'right' way or time.

R U Coming Out inspires, supports and unites those who are living their lives either completely or partially in the closet. The site was set up (and is still run) by Wayne Dhesi in March 2012 while he was a youth worker for the National Health Service. He noticed a gap in support for closeted people and had an idea that gay, lesbian and bisexual people who had come out years ago, and were now content and happy, could share their experiences with those who were struggling with coming out now. The main focus of this website is the stories. People from all over the world write and submit their own personal accounts of coming out. The purpose of the site is not to encourage people to come out before they are ready or to make them feel under any pressure to do things in a particular way; it is simply a source of first-hand accounts from people who have already been through, and are still going through, the process themselves.

R U Coming Out is a really useful tool for parents and friends of those who have come out, offering them accounts from other parents, relatives and friends of gay, lesbian and bisexual people.

All proceeds from this anthology will be given to the RUComingOut charity.
www.rucomingout.com

Printed in Great Britain
by Amazon.co.uk, Ltd.,
Marston Gate.